Ambrose Bierce
and the
One-Eyed Jacks

AMBROSE BIERCE

and the

ONE-EYED JACKS

Oakley Hall

VIKING

VIKING

Published by the Penguin Group

Penguin Putnam Inc., 375 Hudson Street, New York, New York 10014, U.S.A.

Penguin Books Ltd, 80 Strand, London WC2R 0RL, England

Penguin Books Australia Ltd, 250 Camberwell Road, Camberwell,
    Victoria 3124, Australia

Penguin Books Canada Ltd, 10 Alcorn Avenue,
    Toronto, Ontario, Canada M4V 3B2

Penguin Books India (P) Ltd, 11 Community Centre, Panchsheel Park,
    New Delhi- 110 017, India

Penguin Books (N.Z.) Ltd, Cnr Rosedale and Airborne Roads,
    Albany, Auckland, New Zealand

Penguin Books (South Africa) (Pty) Ltd, 24 Sturdee Avenue,
    Rosebank, Johannesburg 2196, South Africa

Penguin Books Ltd, Registered Offices: Harmondsworth, Middlesex, England

First published in 2003 by Viking Penguin, a member of Penguin Putnam Inc.

10 9 8 7 6 5 4 3 2 1

LIBRARY OF CONGRESS CATALOGING-IN-PUBLICATION DATA
Hall, Oakley M.
    Ambrose Bierce and the one-eyed Jacks / Oakley Hall.
        p.   cm.
    ISBN 0-670-03180-1 (alk. paper)
        1. Bierce, Ambrose, 1842–1914?—Fiction. 2. Hearst, William Randolph,
    1863–1951—Fiction. 3. Sausalito (Calif.)—Fiction. 4. Missing persons—Fiction.
    5. Journalists—Fiction. I. Title.
    PS3558.A373 A83 2003
    813'.54—dc21   2002028080

This book is printed on acid-free paper. ∞

Printed in the United States of America
Set in Granjon with Bandicoot display
Designed by Carla Bolte

PROLOGUE

MAGNIFICENT, adj. Having a grandeur or splendor superior to that to which the spectator is accustomed, as the ears of an ass, to a rabbit, or the glory of a glow-worm, to a maggot.

— *The Devil's Dictionary*

MONDAY, APRIL 19, 1891

My performance was to stumble on the slippery deck, cry out, and fall, flailing my arms, over the side of the Southern Pacific Ferry *Santa Rosa.*

It seemed a long way to the water of the bay, during which time I heard the shout of Sam Chamberlain, the editor in chief and stunt manager of the San Francisco *Examiner,* "MAN OVERBOARD!"

I sank into the chill waters, kicking and splashing myself erect, spitting salt water. From the rail of the *Santa Rosa* a frieze of white faces gazed back at me, open mouths shouting. I remembered to kick myself away from the turmoil of white-water created by the side wheel as the ferry drove on past the man overboard, headed for Oakland.

As a journalist employed by the San Francisco *Examiner* for three months now, I had happened to brag that I had spent my youth swimming in the Sacramento River, and so I had been assigned to the *Examiner*'s latest, aquatic stunt. There would be a sensational story about how long it took the SP ferry to rescue a man overboard.

So I floated alone, buoyed by my belt of cork pads. The view from the surface of the bay was not extensive. I could see the masts and smoke of a steamer out toward Alcatraz, Goat Island loomed up behind me, there was no sign now of the *Santa Rosa*. Salt spray splashed in my face from the chop of wavelets. I had loosened my laces aboard, and now I kicked my shoes off. I could feel the drag of water-soaked clothing. I did not permit myself to worry.

I thought of my mother, whose letters lately always concluded with the lines, "Tommy, I am counting on you to give me a grandchild before I grow much older!" and my father, who did not approve of either the *Examiner,* which constantly sought to embarrass his employer, the Southern Pacific Railroad; or my friendship with Ambrose Bierce. I did worry that I would take a cold and not be at my best for the Firemen (I had been a fireman before I was a journalist) in Sunday's baseball game with Acme Drayage.

Hours passed with no rescue. I flipped my hands to keep them warm and maneuver myself to look for signs of a boat coming after me. Chill was settling in my bones when I heard a halloo and saw the mast and sail before I saw the rescue boat itself, Sam Chamberlain leaning over the bow and waving. I divested myself of the cork belt and began thrashing as though in extremis. Sam held up his watch triumphantly.

The rescue had taken fifty-two minutes. I was to write a story of my fall from the slippery deck of the *Santa Rosa* and my very slow rescue for the *Examiner*'s front page, embarrassing the SP Ferry Service, engaging the "gee whiz" emotion in the readership, and increasing the *Examiner*'s circulation in its competition with the *Chronicle*.

The old *Examiner,* which George Hearst had purchased to assist his political career, had been a dreary sheet with advertisements for Cuticura and rupture remedies on the front page. Young Willie Hearst had coaxed his father, the senator, into letting him run the paper, and set out to make it "The Monarch of the Dailies." He contracted with the *New York World* to publish cabled news stories, he chartered trains to deliver the *Examiner* to towns and cities north, south, and east of San Francisco. The circulation rose to surpass that of the *Call,* and engaged in daily battle with Mike de Young's *Chronicle.*

Hearst's salaries were often half again what the other newspapers paid. He hired old friends from the *Harvard Lampoon;* he hired Sam Chamberlain from the New York *World;* he hired Ambrose Bierce, San Francisco's most famous journalist; he hired Winifred Sweet as Annie Laurie, at Sam Chamberlain's recommendation; and he hired me at Bierce's.

The *Examiner*'s news procedures, emulating those of Joseph Pulitzer's *World,* were termed "stunt journalism." A grizzly bear was captured in the wild with weeks of fanfare, and presented to the San Francisco zoo. Annie Laurie pretended to faint on Kearny Street, a boozy patrolman breathed alcohol fumes into her face while sniffing to see if she was drunk. She was packed off to the city hospital to be humiliatingly poked and prodded by smirking interns, dosed with an evil emetic, and released, confirming the reports of city hospital carelessness and mistreatment that had prompted this stunt. The governor of the state immediately fired the hospital staff, and the physician in charge arrived at the *Examiner* seeking satisfaction from Annie Laurie, only to be knocked down by a fellow reporter. Malefactors learned to beware of a redheaded female reporter.

And there was my assignment to the ferryboat gee-whizzer.

The *Examiner* was pro-Democrat, anti–railroad monopoly, pro-labor, and thus anti-Chinese. On Sundays it printed lyrics of popular songs, along with Bierce's column "Prattle."

Murder was always a front-page subject. *Examiner* reporters acted as detectives. Bierce and I had already served together in this respect.

————

Every day at the *Examiner* was filled with the brawl of argument, the ringing of telephones, reporters shouting at editors, and vice versa. Willie Hearst was often so pleased by one of his or one of his editors' ideas that he would burst out of his office and dance a jig in the hall. He was having the time of his life spending the Hearst millions.

However, Willie's father, Senator Hearst, had died in February, and Willie had been shocked by the fact that his father's millions, including the *Examiner,* had been left not to him but to his mother, Mrs. Phoebe Apperson Hearst. Gossip at the *Examiner* had it that the newspaper's high-flying days were numbered, along with those of Willie's Sausalito mistress, Tessie Powers.

————

As though my ducking had been an initiation and my first front-page story my first base hit, that week I found myself treated by the other *Examiner* staff as a regular reporter, with my own cubicle, and not merely as Bierce's assistant. It was just two weeks befoe the Sausalito murders erupted.

At five o'clock on Saturday afternoon, Bierce looked into my office.

"Come, Tom, it is time to tread the Saloon Route. We will celebrate your maritime adventure."

And as we started out, I with a little more swagger than

usual, he said, "It is our consolation in these tiresome times. The untrammeled gloriously independent American saloon!"

The Route led to the numerous saloons on Market Street between 3rd Street and the Palace Hotel or the Montgomery Block, where lavish spreads of food were laid out on the polished counters for the drinkers.

Out on the broad thoroughfare the grand buildings with their ranked tall windows marched east toward the ferries in the scraping din of the street railway cars, the lanes between them clogged with buggies and fringed-top surreys, drays and hacks, all in the clean stench of manure. On the south side of the street a trio of whores paraded in their finery, the ancient newsboy with the long white hair waved an evening newspaper, a balloon seller held up his umbrella of colored balloons. Along the way were crippled beggars and match peddlers, and an organ-player.

A wind had come up, and riding on a current of air, a sheet of newsprint flapped itself high above the traffic. Free as a bird, crumpling and spreading, it fled on down the street.

Our first stop was Guildfoyle's, into the delicious smell of cooked terrapin, cauldrons of the little fellows cooked in the shell in a sauce of butter and sherry. Other saloons had other specialities: crab, turkey, corned beef, game, or ham.

Tall and straight-backed, with sandy graying hair and a noble moustache, Bierce always appeared so clean and laundered that, as someone said, he looked as though he shaved all over. Flower in his buttonhole, with his military gait and stance, he was an aristocratic figure among the gents on the Saloon Route. There among friends his quips or epigrams were usually not so venomous as those that found their way to print in "Prattle."

At Blessington's, the next stop, we encountered a bulldogjowled minister in a backward collar and rusty black suiting who seemed about to attack Bierce with an extended bony finger.

"Mr. Bierce, you have defamed Bishop Runstedt in your column!"

Bierce drew himself up coldly. "You say so, sir?"

"This disrespect for religion cannot be tolerated!"

"I respect religion by having nothing to do with it," Bierce said.

"That is your damnable faithlessness, Mr. Bierce!"

"See here, my man," Bierce said. "No doubt you will say that religion is better than faithlessness. It is not better than faithlessness if it is not true. Truth is better than religion."

"You are bound for hell, Mr. Bierce!" the fellow said, drawing back as though Bierce were to be transported to the infernal regions at this very moment.

"And you for heaven, no doubt," Bierce said. "I tell you that heaven is a prophecy from the lips of despair, while hell is only an inference from an analogy."

He turned away from his flattened opponent and I followed him to the delicacies laid out on the bar. His eyes were flashing.

"What a bunch of hot-gospelers and prayer-worthies they are!" he said. "With their assigned seat in the dress circle of heaven offering a good view of the pit below. Their Jesus Christ was the only man who was ever able to love humankind, for they do not. Nor do I!" he added, and served himself a slice of ham with a generous daub of mustard.

Another fellow presented himself, young and stout with a heft of gold watch chain across his vest. "Mr. Bierce! My wife has charged me to inquire if "Prattle" will not offer us advice on child rearing!"

Bierce looked startled for a moment. Then he touched a finger to his chin, frowning. "Tell her to consider Herod, my good man. Think Herod, sir!"

———

My admiration of Ambrose Bierce ran deep, and at the *Examiner* he was treated like visiting royalty, for it was understood that "Prattle" helped to swell the coffers and allow the high jinks at Willie Hearst's Monarch of the Dailies.

Bierce was the Samuel Johnson of Northern California literature, the Grand Cham of San Francisco. He was a moral and critical monument. His hatred of hypocrisy, cant, and sham and his talent for expressing his indignation at what he called "unworth" made his column so influential that it was often looked on as a kind of Holy Writ. It seemed to me, Tom Redmond, maybe playing Boswell to his Dr. Johnson, that it was not so much what was printed in "Prattle" as the fact that the column carried the moral potency of having been written by Ambrose Bierce.

However, he was also called Almighty God Bierce, from his initials, and not always affectionately.

He had recently published a collection of his stories, *Tales of Soldiers and Civilians*. He was the only major American writer who had actually served in battle in the Civil War, and there was no doubt that his war service had contributed to his misanthropy. I thought his stories admirable, but read all together they left a sour taste. Too many ended with bitter ironies and "twists," too many ended with death, too many of the characters proved Bierce's reasons for despising the human race, and, as Bierce's friend and editor Petey McEwen said of them, "No pretty girl ever appears."

———

In time I had come to realize that although Ambrose Bierce did not try to rein in his own passionate convictions, he was impatient with the convictions of others. He had no sympathy with my own compassion for the oppressed. He took me to task because of a piece I wrote on the slave girls of Chinatown:

In 1869 the *Chronicle* reported a cargo of nine- and ten-year-old Chinese girls as though they were any commodity arrived from the Orient: "The particularly fine portions of the cargo, the fresh and pretty females who come from the interior, are used to fill special orders from wealthy merchants and prosperous tradesmen. Less fine portions of the cargo would be 'boat-girls' from the seaboard towns, where contact with sailors would have reduced their value."

This item was published six years after Abraham Lincoln's Emancipation Proclamation. Not much has changed today, twenty years later, except that the enslaved children are smuggled in among other cargo, and their arrivals are not announced in the newspapers.

The girls are sold at about the age of five by their parents. Syndicates farm as many as eight hundred girls, bringing them along to an acceptable age, at which times prices will be seventy-five or eighty dollars in China. In California, value may rise as high as a thousand dollars, depending upon the degree of attractiveness.

The crib girls on Jackson and Washington streets, and on Bartlett, China, and Church alleys, are exposed like chickens in a cage. Their indentured prostitute contracts are usually for eight years, with two weeks added for each day sick. If they try to escape, their indenture is changed to life.

Girls purchased by "wealthy merchants and prosperous tradesmen" are better off, but they are nonetheless slaves, treated and beaten as slaves, and their indentures are for life, if it can be called life.

At his most pompous, Bierce remarked, "It is not the role of journalists to seek to change God's botchwork world, Tom. Let the poor alone. They are oppressed by no one but their own selves."

CHAPTER ONE

CANNON, n. An instrument employed in the rectification of national boundaries.

— The Devil's Dictionary

TUESDAY, APRIL 27, 1891

Unlike Bierce, my friend Father Flanagan, of Old St. Mary's Cathedral, applauded my piece on the slave girls, and said to me, "I will introduce you to a person who is actually doing something about the plight of those unfortunate children."

Miss Eliza Lindley, directress of the Protestant Stockton Street Mission, was seated at a cluttered desk beneath an elaborate sign that announced: I CAN DO ALL THINGS THROUGH CHRIST WHICH STRENGTHENETH ME. Upstairs was the cheerful racket of the girls the Mission had saved from slavery—"at study," which sounded more like play to me.

Miss Lindley wore severe black-rimmed eyeglasses, a white shirtwaist, and her light brown hair drawn into a bun. She smelled of soap. She ran this place with an iron hand, Father Flanagan had told me. She was a New Englander of granite conscience and devotion to her cause.

"Thank you for your piece in the *Examiner,* Mr. Redmond," she said, rising to proffer her hand. "It was very encouraging to our work here."

"Saving Chinese children's souls," I said.

"And their bodies, Mr. Redmond."

It was the Mission's work to rescue the enslaved children who were worked to the bone by cruel masters and mistresses. She admitted an inability to deal with those who had been imported as the most degraded of prostitutes. Some of their powerful masters were reputed to be white men, and their guardians were armed highbinders.

She was assisted by a teacher of English, Miss Cochran, and a Chinese interpreter. The girls were instructed in American homemaking and female responsibilities in preparation for marriage with reputable gentlemen of their race.

I wanted to see her in action, if that was possible, and she quickly assented. So we went for a walk through the noisy streets of Chinatown, with its powerful smells and brilliant colors and exotic mix of the foreign and the familiar. Miss Lindley seemed very much at home here, in her tight tweed jacket and voluminous skirt. She had removed the spectacles which gave her face a severe expression, and now she looked eager, expectant, and quite pretty, with her high cheekbones and vivid blue eyes. I had to stretch my steps to match the confident stride of her polished black boots.

We halted by a basement entrance beneath an herbalist's shop, where a wraith of a girl was chopping wood. She looked nine or ten, in a filthy white shift, her hair in two untidy braids. She balanced a piece of log on its end, grasped her hatchet with both hands, and brought it down to split off a sliver of the wood. She glanced up at Miss Lindley and quickly away.

"They will claim she is their daughter," Miss Lindley said, as we strode on. "She is not, of course. Did you notice the burns on her arms where they have tortured her?"

"I'm afraid I did not."

"I beg of you that you did," Miss Lindley said, "for we are going before Judge Tallent with that information."

"Does she know who you are?" I asked.

"She knows," Miss Lindley said.

In Judge Tallent's office in Old City Hall I cheerfully perjured myself. A search warrant was issued, a patrolman provided. His name was Perkin and he seemed to be an old friend of Miss Lindley's.

With Miss Lindley leading the way almost at a trot, Perkin hustling behind her in his eight-button blue uniform, we returned to the herbalist's shop. Miss Lindley threw open the basement door. Here were pots boiling over wood fires, in a powerful steaming-vegetable stench. We made our way past clotheslines and hanging garments. A sour-faced Chinaman with a gray beard appeared, calling out, "This velly good house! You go way, Missy Lingling!"

I knew that many of these storefronts concealed gambling establishments and opium dens. Miss Lindley proceeded along a dim passage, sliding her hands over wooden paneling, stooping and stretching. Finally she found something. "Perkin!"

Perkin produced a short iron bar from his pocket, inserted it into a crack, and levered a panel open. Miss Lindley was first inside: a dim room with a lamp burning, a fan-tan layout on a teakwood table, a human squeaking sound. The Chinese child detached herself from an old woman and flung herself into Miss Lindley's arms.

"Perkin! Mr. Redmond!" Miss Lindley said. "Observe that she wears no jewelry. They will come after her for theft."

We observed. The old woman shrieked at us in Chinese. We

departed with the child clinging to Miss Lindley's skirts, this time with Perkin bringing up the rear flourishing his iron bar. We made our way past the malodorous pots and into the light and air.

"My God, Miss Lindley," I called to her. "Do you do this often?"

"She do, mister," Perkin said.

———

Back at the Mission, Miss Lindley showed me the red welts of a recent beating on the child's painfully thin back. The shivering slave girl was turned over to a motherly Chinese woman who rattled at her in her own language and escorted her from the room. Miss Lindley seated herself behind the desk again. A few strands of hair had come loose from her tightly combed coif; her scrubbed face was bright with triumph.

"Well, Mr. Redmond," she said. "Have you enjoyed our foray?"

"Indeed I have!"

"May I summon you if this comes to court?"

"You may."

"And what will you write of us here at the Mission?"

"Just what I have observed."

"Always there is a shortage of money," Miss Lindley said. "Our faithful lawyer, Mr. Duggan, is on one of his infamous drunks again. So we must hire another, who does not serve for the love of a worthy cause."

I asked if I might escort her to dinner.

She directed me to a nearby restaurant replete with golden dragons and red flags. She was very expert in her ordering, and handling her chopsticks. We became friends. I saw that she liked the people among whom she worked, and was loved in return, though I had no doubt she was hated by others. I thought she lived a dangerous life, and one of service to a cause, beyond that of anyone else I knew. At that time I did not know that she often carried a revolver in her reticule.

———

"And were you impressed with Miss Lindley?" Father Flanagan inquired when I met him in the vestry at St. Mary's the next day. He was a short, balding young man in a black cassock with a face so sympathetic you knew that forgiveness was built into his soul.

I said I had been very impressed indeed. "She is a natural wonder."

"She is, unfortunately, a Protestant wonder. She is truly saving souls, Tom, and I do have an impression there is the True Faith somewhere in her background. You must help me to cultivate her."

"Does the Church engage in such rescues?" Do *you,* I meant.

"I wish it did. I'm afraid it requires an indomitable and truly blessed lady such as Miss Lindley. Those poor children trust her; they all know her by some underground railroad of communication. She risks her life, you see. She is offending powerful tong forces."

"I have told her I will write of our adventure," I said.

"You have her permission?"

"I have."

But I wondered how Sam Chamberlain would view my topic.

CHAPTER TWO

SUCCESS, n. The one unpardonable sin against one's fellows.
— *The Devil's Dictionary*

SUNDAY, MAY 2, 1891

I had encountered Miss Winifred Sweet, the *Examiner*'s "Annie Laurie," in the hallways at the newspaper, but had never met her formally until a picnic arranged by Willie Hearst on Angel Island the Sunday after my encounter with Miss Lindley. Boarding Willie's steam launch *Aquila* at the Jackson Street wharf, with a hand from Ah Sook, Willie's Chinese boy, were Miss Sweet, Bierce, Sam Chamberlain, and me. Tessie Powers, Willie Hearst, and another woman were already aboard. It was my first sight of Miss Powers, Willie's mistress, whom he kept in a mansion called Sea Point in Sausalito, across the bay from the City, from which he commuted to the *Examiner* on the *Aquila*. His situation with Miss Powers, and the massive fact of his mother's disapproval of it, were the talk of the *Examiner* staff. He made no effort to keep his liaison a secret, displaying Tessie Powers proudly and publicly. She was a very pretty lady with a shy smile, a face framed with curls and a kind of serenity draped around her like a shawl.

I was surprised to see that the other woman already aboard

was Miss Lindley, her nearsighted face peering unsmiling at me from beneath a black straw bonnet. She wore a tartan cloak over her shoulders.

Willie Hearst was reputed to mount these parties and picnics for selected members of the *Examiner*'s staff for purposes of understanding and cooperation, but seeing Miss Lindley, I understood that she and I had been included in this rather august company because of the latest piece that I had submitted to Sam Chamberlain.

When we chuffed away from the dock, with Ah Sook passing glasses of champagne, Willie Hearst stood stiff-backed and nautically capped at the wheel. He was twenty-eight years old, but he looked much younger, tall and slender with a pink-and-white complexion and a little golden moustache. He was usually slightly diffident in manner except, I observed, aboard the *Aquila,* where he was very much the commander.

He had a high-pitched voice that had refused to grow up with him. He was a good listener, and gave the speaker his full attention, eying him with an unwavering bug-eyed gaze that some found unnerving. His manners were formal: he addressed all his staff as "Mister" and would not allow himself to precede anyone through a doorway.

With dramatic spinnings of the launch's wheel, Willie maneuvered the *Aquila* through the massed hulls of old sailing ships and beneath a thicket of masts and spars into the open bay, the eastern foothills rising to the right, the camel hump of Angel Island straight ahead, and scows under tow to the left, with a high scarf of smoke from the tugboat.

On the noisy passage to Angel Island we were seated in parallel rows on upholstered benches, beneath a varnished canopy, gazing at each other behind Willie Hearst's back. I was seated next to Miss Lindley and Sam Chamberlain beside Miss Powers, but these two ladies were acquainted with each other from back East and frequently chatted across the aisle. Bierce, whom I knew to be cynical about this kind of outing, stood gazing back at the City with his hands clasped behind his back.

Miss Sweet, red-haired and green-eyed, in her crisp cotton blouse and long skirt, had risen from her seat, and rather (I thought) paraded herself, striding up and down with a light step, uttering cries of appreciation at the fancy fittings and upholstery of the *Aquila.* Winnie Sweet had come to the *Examiner* from playing in a traveling theater company of *The Two Orphans,* in which she had impressed Sam Chamberlain.

Miss Powers wore a fluttery blue dress and made some efforts to direct Ah Sook in the passing of the champagne glasses. It was clear that the Chinaman loved his mistress. It was well known that Willie Hearst had collected Miss Powers when he was a student at Harvard. He had brought her west to San Francisco when he had taken over at the *Examiner.*

Feet braced against the motion of the *Aquila,* Miss Sweet complained of the difficulties of writing text for the approval of Mr. Hearst and Mr. Chamberlain.

"Mr. Bierce will no doubt be pleased to instruct you in proper journalistic usage," Willie advised her, turning from his stance at the wheel, his long legs in white flannel trousers spread, hands gripping the gleaming spokes.

I thought that Bierce, who was easy to offend, might be sensitive to this, but apparently he too was impressed by Miss Sweet. Watching him, I thought I would never understand this strange person. Miss Sweet had turned to face him.

"First the necessity of concentrating on the specific rather than the general, my dear," Bierce said.

Miss Sweet's expression as she leaned toward him was all ears.

"'Local man appointed to post,'" he said. "That is a phrase

distinguished by its total lack of information. May I also cite 'a pluvial dispensation,' a term I was disappointed to come across in Monday's *Examiner*?"

He grinned at Willie's back.

"'Rain' is better, you see," he continued, "as it is not pompous and inflated diction. 'Drops battered the leaves of the petunias,' is more effective still. It is visual and aural. There is nothing visual about a 'pluvial dispensation.' Journalism seeks to show, not to impress with the journalist's vocabulary."

"This is very interesting, Mr. Bierce!" Miss Sweet's fidgeting had quieted like a patted colt under Bierce's steady regard.

"You perhaps noticed the verb 'battered' in my previous quotation," Bierce went on. "'Battered' is a strong verb. Strong verbs are more effective than weak verbs bolstered by adverbs. You are cognizant of the parts of speech, Miss Sweet?"

"I am, sir. I was well schooled in Wisconsin."

"'Battered,' you understand, is more effective than 'violently activated,' or 'knocked about wildly.'"

"Yes, I do see!"

"There is a feminine style," Bierce said. "It employs a large dosage of adverbs and adjectives. It is called 'feminine overemphatic.' There is also the feminine fallacy of overmodification. A masculine sentence will usually end with the exclamation mark—if there is to be one—at the end of the sentence. A feminine sentence would have the exclamation mark somewhere in the middle followed by one or two modifying phrases or clauses, if you catch my meaning."

"But, Mr. Bierce, would it not be proper for a feminine journalist to employ a more feminine style than a masculine one, with all those exclamation marks at the end of the sentences?"

Sam Chamberlain let out a whoop of a laugh, and I saw from the stricture of Willie Hearst's nostrils as he turned to glance back at us that he was blocking his own laughter. Miss Powers looked sweetly puzzled. Miss Lindley raised her eyebrows at me, Bierce proffered his glass to Ah Sook for a refill.

"That may be true, Miss Sweet, but the female journalist must not let her nouns and verbs be swamped amongst the multitudinous seas of adverbs and adjectives of the female novelists, such as Mrs. Gertrude Atherton."

That seemed to me to have answered Winnie Sweet's pertness.

"And remember," Bierce said, "only a genius can afford to employ more than one adjective per noun. And that, my dear, only the very choicest."

"Ah, well, Mr. Bierce," Miss Sweet said, straightening and smiling around at the rest of her auditors, "at the *Examiner* I am surrounded by geniuses on every hand—the most outrageous, incredible, ridiculous, glorious set of geniuses one has ever encountered!

"Now, how are those adjectives, Mr. Bierce?"

"Quite perfectly redundant, sentimental, and feminine, Miss Sweet. And charming."

Now everyone was laughing, and Miss Sweet had carried the day. "One perseveres, Mr. Bierce!"

"Perseverance is usually counted a virtue, Miss Sweet. Except in the case of female poets."

More laughter, as Bierce gained the upper hand again.

"Oh, I am not a poet, Mr. Bierce!" Miss Sweet said.

"I am well aware of that, Miss Sweet," Bierce said with a bow.

Miss Lindley said to me in a low voice, "Do you know why I have been invited on this outing, Mr. Redmond?" Her eyes made a slash of intense blue across her face.

I said I thought it had to do with the piece I had written about her and the Stockton Street Mission.

———

Ashore on Angel Island, blankets were spread on a sward above a beach where the *Aquila* rested at anchor. Miss Powers helped Ah Sook heap plates with fried chicken, potato salad, and slaw. Miss Sweet paraded light-footed up and down to show off her figure, and plumped down beside Sam Chamberlain with a pink glow to her cheeks.

She had a gift for focusing the concentration of others, and she entertained us with tales of her two cats Oo-long and So-long. Glancing around at the interested faces, even Ambrose Bierce's, I was conscious of the fatuity of men in the company of an attractive young female.

I estimated the courageous and dedicated Miss Eliza Lindley as worth three of the noisy Miss Winifred Sweet. Miss Powers, because of her situation, could not be gauged in the same way.

I lounged beside Miss Lindley, gazing out at the Golden Gate with the noon sun blazing above it and the line of the horizon visible through it. Ah Sook had distributed large white napkins for wiping chicken grease from our fingers. Willie Hearst, Miss Powers, and Bierce were in conversation ten feet away.

Sam Chamberlain rose to his rickety height and ambled over to seat himself beside me. He was a very fashionably dressed gent, with his high collar, rosy necktie, and gardenia in his buttonhole. Occasionally he would don his monocle to inspect something close at hand.

"Redmond," he said, "Mr. Hearst and I were very taken with your piece on Miss Lindley's adventure in Chinatown. Would you be interested in contributing more of those?"

I would.

"I believe such a series would be useful to your cause, Miss Lindley. Do you agree?"

"I would have to consult my board, Mr. Chamberlain, but I believe they would be enthusiastic."

"Redmond, I must inquire how you would feel if these pieces were to be published above Annie Laurie's byline?"

I blew out my breath. Miss Lindley glanced at me, frowning.

"In her highly adverbial and adjectival style," Sam said quickly. "It may be more fitting, you see."

I did see.

"I think Annie Laurie might make a considerable heroine of Miss Lindley."

"I do not wish to be made a considerable heroine, Mr. Chamberlain," Miss Lindley said.

"In aid of your cause?" Sam asked. "We are thinking of a series. You see, if Miss Sweet were to become active in Chinatown, she would quickly become her own deterrent—a redheaded young woman asking questions. She is already too well known for comfort. Moreover, Miss Sweet will shortly be very involved in the visit of President Harrison to San Francisco. We hope to find a way to introduce her onto the presidential train."

"You want me to write these pieces for her to rewrite in her style?" I said.

He was already nodding.

"I'm a newspaperman," I said. "I am employed by Mr. Hearst. I will do what you tell me to do."

"Thank you, Redmond. You will be suitably rewarded." He leaned past me to address Miss Lindley again.

"You understand that these articles will be anti-Chinese just because they are on the side of the abused children."

"I do understand," Miss Lindley said, but she looked concerned.

The Democratic and Republican newspapers in San Francisco were anti-Chinese because the working class and a majority of the electorate had been so since the depression of 1876. After the completion of the transcontinental railroad, the emigration of the Chinese railroad workers to San Francisco had depressed the labor market. Not many years ago Dennis Kearney and the sandlotters would build up a Sunday head of steam shouting anti-Chinese denunciations at each other, which often resulted in a mob effort to set fire to Chinatown. While this no longer happened, the sentiment remained. With Miss Lindley, however, I was on the side of the orphans.

"And you will discuss the matter with the board of the Mission?"

"I will do so as soon as possible," Miss Lindley said.

"We will have some whizzes of stories," Sam said. He beckoned to Miss Sweet, and she swept over to seat herself beside Miss Lindley. In this conference on the news articles that were to be written, Miss Sweet was no longer the pert and flighty young person she had seemed aboard the *Aquila;* she had become an all-business journalist. For the first time I was impressed by her person. It was decided that she would accompany Miss Lindley the next day on a court appearance having to do with a rescued child, but after that the initial writing would be left to me.

———

Later, when Miss Sweet, Miss Powers, and Sam Chamberlain had gone for a walk, Miss Lindley said to me, "I think your employers are using you rather shamelessly, Mr. Redmond."

"Worthy cause."

"I'm afraid the *Examiner*'s interest may offend the Sam Yups."

The Sam Yups was the tong currently controlling Chinatown.

I looked into her eyes. "The feeling I had, Miss Lindley, when I came away from our last meeting, was that you are afraid of nothing."

She flushed and looked down. "That is very kind, Mr. Redmond, but I am often frightened. May I call you Tom?"

"If I may call you Eliza."

Just then the three hikers were profiled on the ridge against the brilliant sun, a young woman attached to each of Sam Chamberlain's arms. They made a delightful picture there, the tall thin man between the two pretty women with their faces shaded by their hat brims. The sun made a kind of halo around Miss Powers, whose dress fluttered in a little breeze coming in from the ocean. Miss Sweet was laughing and gesturing, and stepping along beside Sam neat-footed as a pony.

Bierce joined Eliza and me, not quite so sartorially splendiferous as Sam Chamberlain, but well-outfitted all the same, in a black suit with a blossom in the buttonhole. "So they have talked you into it, Tom."

"They have."

"Willie must have his gee-whiz stories. Are you content with this endeavor, Miss Lindley?"

"I am confident of Mr. Redmond's efforts, Mr. Bierce."

"So you should be," Bierce said.

Presently it was time to depart, the others stood, Ah Sook gathering up the plates and stowing them in a basket. I rose to my feet, and Eliza extended her cool hand to me for assistance, smiling up into my face.

————

When the *Aquila* had delivered us back to the Jackson Street wharf, we parted company, and Eliza and I set off for Stockton Street in a hack.

On Kearny Street the fancy cast-iron facades marched away

before us, along with stacked columns of bay windows. On a telephone line before Mrs. Warner's parlor house intimate garments were draped as an advertisement, a pink silk chemise doubled over the wire, and a short shift with long sleeves pinned out like a flying figure.

Eliza said, "I have been invited to a grand ball aboard one of the steam yachts in Sausalito next Saturday. I wonder if I may beg you to escort me."

"Certainly," I said.

"I'm afraid I have been asked because of a certain notoriety of my occupation, and I would be much more comfortable with a stalwart person beside me."

I was very pleased to be her escort, and it was at this rather grand affair that the second of the Sausalito murders that were to occupy Ambrose Bierce and me for the ensuing weeks was to occur.

CHAPTER THREE

ADMONITION, n. Gentle reproof, as with a meat-axe. A friendly warning.

— *The Devil's Dictionary*

SATURDAY, MAY 8, 1891

Lights from the *Oriana* rippled over the wavelets of the bay like bright cloth, masts disappearing into the high night. The cliffs of Sausalito rose behind us, dotted with sparse lights, which illuminated Eliza's upright figure seated in the stern of the little taxi boat that had brought us out from the Yacht Club dock. The boatman eased his craft against the float beside August Larkyn's steam yacht. I took Eliza's hand to help her onto the float.

Along with a trio of pretty and fancy-gowned young women from San Francisco, we trooped down a noisy hardwood deck to a lighted maw that led below.

Eliza was in a severe mood: "Young women are lured to these parties aboard the yachts," she had said. "They come over from the City to be feted and champagned, the yachts tour the bay, then it is discovered that the tide has gone out, and the yacht cannot return to its anchorage—so the night must be spent. It is well known, but still they come, unchaperoned.

Who are they? Daughters of doctors, merchants, and tradesmen, but also working young women in their best finery. It is a disreputable business, and August Larkyn is the worst offender.

"Important people have been invited tonight," she added. "I am sure there will be no tours of the bay and running aground on mud banks."

"And you are invited as the directress of the Stockton Street Mission?"

"August Larkyn thinks he may make a friend of me. He is one of those men who cannot bear dislike or disapproval. Or else his sense of humor is as perverted as his interests."

She took my arm as we crossed the deck.

We descended into the ballroom where the flames of the wall sconces gleamed on the polished floor and on the bare arms and half-bare bosoms and bright faces and white shirtfronts of the assembled important people. The first step into the ballroom was a stagger from the list of the yacht which, at low tide, rested on a cradle of mud.

And there was Captain Larkyn before us, stout in his double-breasted navy blue jacket and white trousers, with his cap of reddish hair which had turned white at the temples, and his red laughing cheeks of welcome. It was like being greeted by the Union Jack.

"Ah, it is the bonny Miss Eliza Lindley!" he said, flinging his arms out as though to embrace Eliza in them. When she retreated a step, one of his hands came around with a clever serpentine motion to shake mine in a quick flip of disinterest as Eliza introduced me.

"How d'ye do, Mr. Redmond?"

"And you, sir?" I said.

"And will we be seeing any of your charges here tonight, Miss Lindley?"

"I am certain that you will not, Captain Larkyn."

With a laugh, Larkyn dance-stepped away to greet a couple of young ladies, and Eliza and I moved toward the punch bowl, our pace accelerated by the slant of the floor. The wooden walls, deck, and overhead magnified the din of conversation like the reflections of the lights.

"He seems charming enough," I said.

"He is a charming defiler of foolish young women," she said grimly.

No doubt the beautiful white steam yacht was a great enhancement to this hobby. It seemed to me that there was some sort of metaphor in the fact that this elegant ballroom was set on a perceptible slant.

"What did he mean—will any of your charges be here? Is that a joke?"

"He is aware that I counsel certain young women who are not children. Women of his acquaintance." To change the subject, she said, "Oh, there are Mr. Hearst and Miss Powers!"

Willie Hearst was in perfect soup and fish, fair hair parted in the middle, and a wisp of moustache. Miss Powers, on his arm in a gray gown, showed a good deal of bosom. Her pretty face was surrounded by a swarm of ringlets.

"We knew each other in Cambridge," Eliza said of Miss Powers. "I was so surprised to meet her again. How pretty she is!"

It was interesting to me that Eliza disapproved of Captain Larkyn as a womanizer, but did not disapprove of Miss Powers.

Willie Hearst raised a hand in greeting, and had started toward us with Tessie when he was halted by a group of young people swirling around them. A small orchestra had assembled on a dais on the far side of the room, and it now began to play. The music and murmur of many conversations pulsed together.

"Do you waltz, Tom?" Eliza inquired, removing her eyeglasses and storing them in her reticule. We waltzed. She was a better dancer than I, as all women seemed to be. When the waltz was over her face was flushed and smiling.

"That was very nice!" she said.

I was still breathing a little hard from my exertions, but I could honestly agree with her.

I had been wondering why she and I were here, and now I smiled to think that it might be because this stern and sturdy savior of the Chinese slave girls loved waltzing.

"Were you aware in Cambridge that Miss Powers and Willie Hearst were associated?" I asked.

"It was well known," Eliza said, and excused herself to tend to feminine matters.

Sausalito was considered foreign, exotic, a bit racy. The notorious yachting set was mainly British: three big steam yachts, plus Willie's *Aquila,* and five or six lesser sailers. There were also more staid and conservative members of the British colony, businessmen and merchants who were not yachtsmen, and an even more conservative, Catholic settlement of Portuguese fisherman around the bend from the yacht harbor.

Captain Larkyn's voice could be heard above the music as he greeted newcomers on the steps down from the deck. I noticed that Willie, watching him, wore a scowl on his boyish face. He and Miss Powers were not dancing.

I made my way up the slant to join a fellow journalist named Orlow Black, a handsome young fellow who was losing his cottony hair. He was interested in the *Examiner* and Hearst.

"Hoping to get on there, you know, Tom."

Black presently practiced his profession at the *Call.* Like many local journalists he would rather be working for Hearst for better pay. Others, however, were shocked by the *Examiner*'s harum-scarum tactics and disregard for facts.

He was well acquainted with Sausalito, Black said.

"I understand Willie Hearst has a regular photographic workshop set up over here," I said. "When he goes after a thing he goes whole hog."

Nodding, Black said, "Photographer named Billings in charge. There's a young man who poses doing all kinds of physical business. Billings works with banks of cameras so this fellow can be seen almost as though he is in motion. Poses nude, I heard."

Black jerked his chin, pointing. "His name is James Dix. Wonder why he's here."

I wondered why Black was here, along with Eliza and myself. It seemed a strangely mixed bag of an affair.

James Dix was a rather ordinary-looking young man with black hair combed close to his scalp and broad shoulders. Arms folded on his chest, he was conversing with one of the young women who had arrived on the same ferry as Eliza and I. Many dancers were circling the floor now.

Tessie Powers was a more pleasing sight than the model Dix. Her pale face slanted from high cheekbones to a tiny chin. The visible flesh of her bosom gleamed like lilies. She clung to her protector's arm. Watching the dancers, the pair seemed to be alone in the crowd. I said so to Black.

"She's disapproved of. The Brits over here call her 'dirty drawers.'"

"What do they mean by that?"

"Her *situation*."

I looked around for Eliza, who was gone a long time. Captain Larkyn was greeting newcomers with wide-armed motions of welcome.

"Regular Don Juan, as I hear it," Black said. "One-eyed jacks."

"One-eyed jacks?"

"What they call these yachts gents over here. But Larkyn can be very personable."

I saw that Captain Larkyn had climbed the steps to speak to someone in the outer darkness.

There was a yell, a shot, a shout, a scream. Larkyn stepped carefully backward down the stairs, one step, another, then he toppled flat over backward and fell with a sickening whack audible over the sound of the music.

That was the end of Captain Larkyn's ball.

———

Back on the Yacht Club dock, under the shifting lights gleaming through the blown branches, we waited for the boats to come in from the *Oriana,* which blazed with light a hundred yards out in the bay. Two of the other yachts were also lit up. Guests from the *Oriana* huddled in groups along the dock, each boatload's passengers standing separate from the others.

Willie Hearst and Tessie Powers had climbed steps that disappeared into darkness. Eliza, clutching her wrap around her shoulders, paced beside me. She had scarcely spoken since the murder of Captain Larkyn.

Her reticule glanced off my leg.

"What have you got in there?" I asked, rubbing the place.

Before she could answer, a cloaked figure came up beside her. A girl's face glanced up at Eliza from beneath a hood.

"What happened, Miss Lindley?"

"He's dead. Shot dead."

There was a gasp. *"Who did that?"*

"I don't know, my dear."

I was introduced to Isabella da Costa. A very young, beautiful, intense face, pink buds of lips, and dark eyes that gazed into mine for an instant. I saw the motion within her cloak; she had crossed herself.

"So you decided to attend, my dear," Eliza said. "You are a little late. And you told me you would not."

"He sent me a note," the girl whispered. "He—I'm sorry!" she said, and was gone, a slim figure in a full-length purple cloak fading into the shadows as she hurried away.

"What a beautiful child," I said.

"Not a child. She will be queen of the Festa in June. It's a Portuguese celebration of the Holy Ghost here in Sausalito."

"She is one of your charges?"

"Yes." She paced, a shape like an elongated hourglass in her long skirts, tight jacket, and hat.

"I advised her not to attend tonight," she continued. "I advised her that she is in grave danger."

"From Larkyn?"

"Yes."

I turned to watch the lights of the *Oriana* blinking across the water.

"Would that be why you are carrying a gun, Eliza?"

"I have a gun," she said. "There have been threats. Yes, Tom," she said.

"Has it been fired?" I asked.

I heard the shocked suck of her breath. She bent her head to fumble in her bag. She handed a heavy Colt Peacemaker to me. I flipped the cylinder on its crane and felt for the cartridge slots, all empty but one. The metal was cold; it had not been fired.

"Why?" I asked.

"I intended to show it to him."

"But you didn't."

"There was no occasion."

"A threat on your part," I said.

"Yes."

"On behalf of Isabella da Costa?"

"On behalf of the female gender. Never mind it, please, Tom."

Aboard the gleaming *Oriana* the Sausalito chief of police and a skinny patrolman were doing whatever they were doing. I handed Eliza back the revolver, which she returned to her reticule.

A tall figure approached us, with a gleam of the overhead lights on his reddish, fairish moustache. It was Bierce.

CHAPTER FOUR

INCOMPATIBILITY, n. In matrimony a similarity of tastes, particularly the taste for domination.

— *The Devil's Dictionary*

SATURDAY, MAY 8, 1891

As Bierce and I walked along the quay, I told him what had happened aboard the *Oriana,* keeping the fact of Eliza's Peacemaker to myself. She had not protested when she had been put aboard the ferry to return to San Francisco, understanding that Bierce and I were now working journalist-detectives on the track of a major story.

"I am very suspicious of coincidences," Bierce said.

"What do you mean?"

"Our employer has asked me to investigate some mysterious circumstances at Sea Point. I wonder if this shooting you have described is not related."

"Does it have to do with photography?" I inquired.

He looked at me in surprise. "Indeed it does! Photographic plates have been stolen. I assume they are photographs of Miss Powers in a natural state, although Willie Hearst has not said as much."

"Dirty drawers," I said.

"What's that?"

I explained.

"I think 'no drawers' may be the actual case," Bierce said.

"I understand there is an in-house photographer," I said.

"Willie believes it will become possible to print photographs in newsprint. He and Jasper Billings are also interested in photographing motion."

I told Bierce about James Dix; he nodded when I mentioned the name.

"He has been photographed in motion, in the nude, to show the working of muscles. I suspect that Miss Powers has been similarly employed. Willie wants me to help recover the missing plates."

I recounted my conversation with Orlow Black. We turned to retrace our steps. The light reflections which brightened the paving stones turned the shadows darker.

I said, "I did not see who shot Captain Larkyn, but I did see who did not. Neither Miss Powers nor Willie Hearst nor James Dix were out of my sight."

"There may be some connection between Captain Larkyn and the missing plates."

"He had an interest in female flesh. He and some of the other yachtsmen over here are called the one-eyed jacks."

"I assume that refers to penile gentry," Bierce said, pacing beside me.

————

We climbed brick steps that wound up the hillside to Sea Point, where electric lights illuminated a broad veranda. Lighted higher stories merged into foliage and shadow. Ah Sook, in a white jacket, let us in, murmuring greetings. Seated in the slipcovered chairs on the veranda were Willie Hearst, rising, and Miss Powers, between them a low table on which were two small stemmed glasses and a candle in a silver holder.

Hearst greeted me with his limp handshake and intense

gaze. "You and your journalistic subject Miss Lindley attended that tragic affair tonight, Mr. Redmond?"

"Yes, sir."

Miss Powers offered me a sweet smile. The curls clustered around her triangular face made it resemble a valentine.

"As you know, Mr. Hearst, Mr. Redmond has assisted me in previous investigations," Bierce said. "He has now been a witness to the murder of Captain Larkyn."

"Miss Powers and I were also witnesses," Willie said.

We were presented with chairs, and seated ourselves. Willie Hearst signaled to Ah Sook to bring two more glasses, into which he poured liqueur. Tessie Powers watched all this with worried eyes.

"If you do not mind reviewing the situation again, Mr. Hearst," Bierce said.

Willie said in his high voice, "Yesterday Mr. Billings reported the set of plates missing. He had no idea when they disappeared—it must have been within a week or so, he thinks."

"And they are immodest photographs of Miss Powers?"

"They are photographs of Miss Powers running, carrying various objects, stepping over a footstool, reaching up, swinging an Indian club. She is unclothed, because it is Mr. Billings's project to photograph the musculature of the human body in its locutions. His ambition is to photograph bodies in motion, you understand."

In the candlelight it was as though a pink shadow had swept up Tessie Powers's face. Her smile had disappeared.

"How many of them were there?"

Willie glanced at Miss Powers, who said in her whisper, "About fifteen."

"And were they identified in some way?"

"They were in a wooden box with a white card with my name on it tacked to the side."

"It would seem, then, that someone broke into the photographic studio with that box in mind."

"Yes," Tessie whispered.

"And who might that have been, Miss Powers?" Bierce glanced my way to show me that these questions were for my benefit.

"I don't know!"

"Is there any connection with Captain Larkyn?" I asked.

She seemed to sink deeper into her chair.

"Yes, there is," Willie said. "Larkyn has been very forward with her. She did not wish to attend tonight's affair for that reason."

One-eyed jacks and dirty drawers. Tessie's role in Willie Hearst's household was suggestive and perhaps full of promise, even if in person she was modest and even demure.

"Miss Powers and I are not married," Willie said. "For that reason she has had to endure a great deal of disapproval." He shook his head once. "Captain Larkyn has made—suggestions."

"He invited me to take lunch with him aboard the *Oriana,*" Miss Powers said.

Bierce knitted his fingers together. "So it might be construed that Larkyn could have stolen the photographic plates to give himself a certain position."

I wondered why Willie and Miss Powers had attended Captain Larkyn's ball. I thought of Eliza Lindley with the Peacemaker in her reticule, and of Tessie Powers embarrassed by the evidence of her immodesty. There seemed to be a gee-whiz story here, but not one designed for Miss Sweet's adjectives and adverbs.

"Tell me," Bierce said. "Where is Jasper Billings now? Was he also aboard the *Oriana?*"

"He declined. He is very engrossed in his work. He might be in the darkroom at this moment."

"May we determine if that is the case?"

Willie rose and strode inside the darkened house, where his voice could be heard on some kind of communication device. He returned to say, "There is no answer. But he doesn't answer if he is in the darkroom."

We trooped upstairs together, Miss Powers trailing. The photographic studio spanned most of the north side of the house. Electric lights gleamed on brass fittings on cameras on tripods, and on broad counters on which rested mysterious machinery and stacks of large gray albums. Willie walked to a door over which there was a brass plaque that announced DARKROOM. He rapped and called out, "Mr. Billings!" He pushed the door open to darkness, and reached up to twitch a cord. The room came alight. There was an acid stink.

"Oh, my gracious, he's fainted!" Willie said. "Mr. Billings!"

He turned a pale face to Bierce and me, and moved on into the darkroom to bend over the man who lay on the floor.

"Oh, my God!" Willie said. He straightened quickly. "He's dead!"

Miss Powers emitted a muffled shriek.

The body was that of a balding man in his shirtsleeves and a denim apron, crumpled on the parquet with his shoulder against a cabinet. Blood had dried on the side of his head. Bierce stood looking down at him.

Willie and I moved the corpse, which was very stiff, out into the other room. Bierce stooped to pick up a photographic plate that had been concealed by the body. The acid stink wafted out of the darkroom. Tessie Powers stood with her back turned. Outside the windows was the black vastness of the bay, with a speckle of lights along the far Oakland shore.

"He must have fainted, and fallen and hit his head—" Willie said.

"I think not," Bierce said.

He held the photographic plate up to the light, then passed it to Willie, who briefly examined it before handing it to me. It was a picture of a young woman, unclothed except for a kind of veil over one shoulder and covering one thigh. A breast was exposed. She was smiling, fair-haired, quite pretty. She was seated on a column on which was, in raised large print, the name AGLAIA.

"What is this?" Bierce demanded.

Willie didn't know.

"Aglaia is one of the Graces," Bierce said. "There are three of them. Were you one, Miss Powers?"

Hand covering her mouth and chin, dark eyes wide, Miss Powers shook her head.

"Are you sure, Tessie?" Willie demanded.

She continued to shake her head, her eyes fixed on the body of the photographer Jasper Billings.

"I think someone hit him very hard on the right temple with a blunt instrument," Bierce said. "It appears that the bludgeon was brought here for that purpose, since there is nothing in the darkroom that would have served."

"Why, please?" Willie asked, standing and rubbing his hands together as though they were cold.

"Why was Captain Larkyn shot? Billings was brained first, I would think."

"Photographs," I said.

"Poor Jasper, that sweet man!" Tessie cried. "Who will notify his poor mama, Willie?"

"I will do that," Willie Hearst said.

CHAPTER FIVE

DEBAUCHEE, n. One who has so earnestly pursued pleasure that he has had the misfortune to overtake it.
— *The Devil's Dictionary*

SUNDAY, MAY 9, 1891

On the deck of the *Oriana* the next afternoon, Bierce, Chief Casey of the Sausalito Police, and I gazed down the steps that led to the ballroom, where Captain Larkyn's murderer had stood to fire the shot that had killed him. A patrolman in an unpressed uniform was stationed at the head of the gangplank.

"There was some light," Casey said. "But nobody saw anything. Appears like everybody was down in the ballroom place."

"What about crew?" Bierce asked. "A yacht like this must have a considerable crew."

"Takes a crew of fifteen when it is ocean bound, I understand, but when it is anchored up here, there's only four, as I can make out. There's a fellow name of Croft that's the mate, a valet kind of person name of Pearson, and a couple of seamen-fellows. 'Course for the grand ball there was servant staff hired for the occasion."

Casey was a lean-jawed, disjointed-looking fellow with a

half-grown stubble of beard and a kind of apologetic slouch. He wore a battered cap that was more maritime than police, and a blue uniform.

"Tell me," Bierce said. "How long has the *Oriana* been moored here at the Yacht Club?"

"Oh, long time," Casey said. "Four, five, six years. I'll find that out for you, Mr. Bierce."

"And the other big yachts are British also," Bierce said, pointing to the several yachts in the anchorage flying Union Jacks.

"Well, that's the *Circe,* Captain Jones," Casey said. "And that's Captain Bastable's *Evelyn Wright.* Captain Corey's *Rambler.* Captain Peavine's *Clio.*"

"These are the men known as the 'one-eyed jacks'?"

Casey produced an embarrassed grimace. "Well, not Corey, I reckon, he's a good fambly man, wife and children in a house on the hill. Well, and not Charley Peavine either."

"Is the 'jacks' for Union Jacks?" I asked.

"I don't know that, Mr. Redmond."

"These are the social leaders of the British colony here?"

"Well, they're the ones get the most notice, Mr. Bierce. There's other Brits that's not such swells, if you understand me. Merchants and such. Good citizens, regular folks."

We proceeded to the captain's quarters in the stern of the yacht. A band of windows gave expansive views, past the yacht *Circe,* of the sparkling bay and San Francisco's sand hills gleaming in the afternoon sun.

Bierce stood militarily erect with a finger pressed to his chin, glancing around him.

The port side of the cabin held a canopied bed with a white ruffled coverlet, a chest of drawers, a wooden sea chest. The starboard side was the office, with a desk three-quarters the size of the bed and an oak filing cabinet. Beneath our feet was an Oriental rug laid on a bias.

"To whom does possession of the *Oriana* pass?" Bierce inquired.

"There's fambly in England—London, England," Casey said. "His friend Captain Bastable's been in touch. Says they don't seem to be studying on coming out here."

"Disapproved of Larkyn?" Bierce asked.

"Wouldn't be for me to say," Casey said.

Bierce frowned at him. The muted pat of waves beneath us was soothing.

"Maybe," Casey added.

"Tom, you take a look through the bureau," Bierce said, and I complied. The top drawer was divided in half, stockings to the right and a collection of metal studs, cuff links, and a gold watch fat as a turnip to the left.

Bierce opened the top drawer of the file cabinet, Casey watching him uneasily.

I uncovered the photographic album in the bureau's second drawer, beneath folded undergarments. Bierce laid it open on the desk. The first page revealed a female face, in a photograph clipped to the page with small black decorative corner brackets.

"Who is this young beauty?" Bierce asked, to no response.

She was a pretty girl, no doubt of that—high forehead under a valence of dark curls, large eyes, a prim little mouth, some discreet display of bosom above a fringe of lace.

"A conquest?" I wondered.

Casey made a disapproving sound. Bierce unclipped the photograph and regarded the writing on the reverse. "Antonia Larkyn," he said. "Daughter, I imagine."

There were more photographs of young women in the album, not so discreetly garbed. The photo of Larkyn's daughter, if that was who she was, heading this collection made me uneasy, as though there were ancient European evils and perversities I could scarcely imagine.

"Conquests was what Captain Larkyn were all about," Casey said. "Fair to him to say they was after him about the same rate of push as he was them. I will say it took me poorly to see that evening ferry coming in with a new crop of young ladies setting out for them levees aboard this boat, and who knows what else. *Circe* and *Evelyn Wright* about as bad. Well, not as bad."

"Celebration of the difference between the genders," Bierce said.

"No doubt, sir."

I paged through the book, maybe twenty photographs. A few of the young faces seemed dimly familiar, but nothing I could lay name or place to. At the back of the album was a large attached envelope containing five more photographs.

My breath came hard as I realized that one of these was Eliza Lindley, or a twin sister, gazing provocatively over a bare shoulder. I hurried to stuff the five back into their envelope.

"One may surmise that the man was murdered because of one of these females," Bierce said. "Therefore they must be identified. Can this be accomplished, Chief? The manservant?"

"Well, sir, looks like Ben Pearson has cleared out," Casey said. "There's the mate, however, Jackie Croft."

"We'll want to see him."

Casey nodded. I was still shaky from the photograph of Eliza.

"There must have been a social secretary who sent out invitations for this social ball?"

Casey looked surprised. "That'd been Mrs. Grayling. I'll look into it," he said, and took up the album with its photograph of Eliza Lindley, who had attended the fatal ball aboard the *Oriana* with a revolver in her purse.

I went back to the bureau while Bierce continued to search through the drawers of the file cabinet. Casey must not have made such a search, and in fact he was watching us with his fingers knitted together anxiously.

Bierce found a tan envelope containing the photographs of Tessie Powers in the bottom drawer.

He laid the eight photographs out on the desktop as though dealing a poker hand. Four of them were "naughty" photographs, no doubt of that, but Tessie, although she was naked, was holding up a box in what was a perfectly mundane image. Her body was as pale as marble, and this photograph showed perfect breasts neither displayed nor concealed, the length of thigh with a smooth stretch of muscle flexed, a tiny delta of private hair discreetly glimpsed. The photograph was perfectly tasteful, and the body exposed was breathtakingly perfect, topped by a demure but serious countenance with a cap of curls. Willie Hearst's pride and affection for his mistress was understandable.

I was still so jangled by the photograph of Eliza I could hardly get my thoughts together.

Bierce said to me, "This may not even have been stolen from Sea Point." Fifteen plates, Tessie Powers had said.

Casey's face was pink with embarrassment. "Well, I have disapproved of this gent as long as I have known of him," he said with his lips sucked in grimly. "This fellow surely got what was coming to him, I say, though I will pursue his murderer with all the powers I possess." He folded his arms on his chest, gripping the photo album in them, and glared from me to Bierce.

Bierce said, "I take it that the young women in the album are not local ladies, or you would recognize them."

"That is correct," Casey said.

"But I must believe his seductions were not all from across the bay."

"Some were here," Casey said.

"Ah!"

"One of the other yacht fellows," Casey said. "Charley Peavine. Curly-haired, curly beard fellow. He was not one of these nasty-minded gents pursuing those young women coming over on the ferries. But there was talk he would meet with a band of local folks up in the hills. There would be music and dancing and liquor drunk, and lewd behavior. I never saw it, you understand, but it was gossip in town here some years back. Not just young single women, either."

But you don't class him as a one-eyed jack?"

"Different sort. Him and Larkyn wasn't friends, I know that."

"Lewd behavior in the hills," Bierce said. "Did you not take it seriously, Chief?"

"Thought it was more talk than a actual thing. Though now I am thinking about it different. All these young ladies. Seems to me that some young ladies is as randy as young gents."

"A shocking theory," Bierce said, but I saw he was amused. "Is there someone I might talk to who might have been present at these events in the hills, Chief?"

"Might as well talk to Charley Peavine hisself," Casey said.

Nodding, Bierce said to me, "Somewhere here, Tom, I believe we will find a more pertinent stock of photographs."

I found them in a cedar box affixed among the bedsprings, which opened with a concealed latch on the bedrail. There were two stacks of photos, about 4 by 6 inches, fastened together with rubber bands. These appeared to be the girls of the album in wanton and unclothed poses. None of these were Eliza Lindley or Tessie Powers. The other stack was all of one girl, a dark-haired, dark-eyed beauty, arrayed against the stripes of an American flag, all in the same or only slightly differing pose, with her face below her eyes concealed in a kind of Moroccan half-veil,

When Bierce took this stack from me and flipped the edges,

the girl came into motion and stiffly danced. The grotesquerie of the dance was so different from the innocence of the half-concealed face that the performance was shocking.

"Willie said Billings had been trying to perfect a method of photographing motion," Bierce said. He showed the riffled motion of the dark-haired girl to Casey. "Is this a local young lady?"

"Don't know her," Casey said gruffly, red-faced. I thought that part of his embarrassment was that his own search had failed to uncover this photographic trove.

Also in the compartment was a sheepskin condom stretched over a large wooden spool.

"Dear Lord!" Casey said.

————

Casey took charge of the several collections of photographs, and Bierce and I settled in a saloon opposite the wharfs, where he ordered a bourbon and I a pilsener. When I brought up the subject of Willie's mother, Bierce described being summoned to a meeting that morning at the *Examiner* with the lady, Mrs. Senator George Hearst.

She was a very small individual, he said, wrapped in a quantity of expensive woven material, bonneted and carrying an umbrella against an inclement day. He invited her to seat herself, and she did so, wrapping a quantity of yardage around her legs and bracing her umbrella against the arm of her chair.

She fixed him with a disapproval of countenance and a weight of eye that would have disturbed Commodore Vanderbilt. Or George Hearst, of whom it was said that the scorpion that stung him on the testicles had died in convulsions.

"Mr. Bierce," she had said. "You are my son's friend."

"And employee, madam," Bierce replied.

"You are aware then of the person of Miss Powers, who occupies my son's household, and in fact his personal quarters."

Bierce was so aware.

"Of whose presence in his life I entirely disapprove," Mrs. Hearst said.

"That is common knowledge, madam."

"And now my son's photographer, Mr. Billings, has been murdered."

"Yes, murder, madam," Bierce said.

"Who was the author of some photographs taken of Miss Powers in an unclad state. Lewd photographs, Mr. Bierce!"

"Indeed they are not!" Bierce said, and explained the photographs that had been taken of Miss Powers.

"Nevertheless they will constitute a scandal as connected with the death of Mr. Billings."

Bierce admitted that that might be so.

"Your son is interested in photography as it may be employed in the newspaper," he told her. "And Mr. Billings was interested in photographing bodies in motion. I believe these photographs are of scientific intent."

"Mr. Bierce, you will understand my point of view, which is to avoid a scandal involving my son."

"Indeed," Bierce said, and propped his fingertips together, gazing at Mrs. Hearst over them.

"Mr. Bierce, I will ask your assistance in ending this scandalous alliance in which William is involved."

"Your son's infatuation may be foolish, madam," Bierce said, "but I can assure you that it is genuine. I will be party to no such thing."

"Yet you claim to be his friend, sir!"

"That is a conundrum to which you must allow me my own solution, madam."

She sighed, and her face relaxed from its expression of severity. "Ah, well, Mr. Bierce, I will hope, however, that you will do what you can to keep this matter from falling on William's head."

"Yes, I will!" Bierce said.

With activity something like unwrapping a package, she laid aside the folds of her skirt, settled her bonnet, took up her reticule and umbrella and rose, like some grand blossom unfolding in the sunlight, made a motion like a half a curtsy, and departed.

Bierce said he felt as though the team and dray bearing down on him on Market Street had veered aside at the last moment.

CHAPTER SIX

PRICE, n. Value, plus a reasonable sum for the wear and tear of conscience in demanding it.
— *The Devil's Dictionary*

TUESDAY, MAY 11, 1891

Chief Casey had arranged meetings with the *Oriana* mate Jack Croft, Billings's photographic subject James Dix, and the reveler Captain Charles Peavine in the Bon Ton Saloon across the esplanade from the wharves of Sausalito.

Croft was a weasel-faced man with a nautical cap, which, removed, exposed a scalp as bald and spotty as an ostrich egg. He had a way of leaning an arm on the table and craning his neck to look Bierce or me straight in the face that made me want to lean back away from him.

"So, Mister Croft," Bierce said. "You claim you were not aboard the *Oriana* when Captain Larkyn was shot."

"That be correct, sir," Croft said, peering into Bierce's face as though to convince him by sheer eye power. "Made a trip to the dock for more of the bubbly. Captain Larkyn was apt to concern himself with things running out. Come back to all the milling and shouting."

"And have you any suppositions as to the identity of the murderer?"

49

Croft moved back a bit so he had room for a powerful shrug. "Ah, where to look, eh? Husbands! Paters!" He laughed unconvincingly.

"More paters than husbands, I would suppose," Bierce said. "Pretty young things come over on the ferry to meet a genuine gold-plated yachtsman."

Croft produced the dubious laughter again. "That would be correct, sir!"

"Who was the photographer?" I asked.

He switched his pose, arm on the table, chin on his bicep, eyes fixed on mine. The pupils danced nervously. "Many photogs about," he said. "Mr. Hearst had one lived upstairs from him."

"What others?"

"Ah, dunno that!"

"Some of the photographs were taken in the cabin," Bierce said. "There would have been cumbersome equipment, none of which was aboard. The camera, a tripod, magnesium flares. You must have observed some of this activity."

"Swear to God," Croft said, with his thin-lipped smile. He leaned on the table.

Bierce moved his glass out of range.

"But you were aware of young women in that cabin?"

"Oh, surely," Croft smirked. "Sweet young persons! Such dee-lightable smells!"

I thought I would have to go for a bath after this interview.

"Was anyone else involved in these tête-à-têtes in the cabin?"

"Dunno if Captain Bastable didn't come over sometimes. Him and Augie Larkyn was old pals." Struck by a thought, he raised a finger like a candle. "Come to remember! There was a young fellow brought some big truck with him—maybe it was these cameras and such."

"A young fellow," Bierce said.

"Young fellow with a big hat. Choirboy face to him!"

"Did you have any duties to do with these sessions, sir?"

"Mate of the ship, not the bedworks." He laughed again.

"What other crew was there?"

"Jink Ratched and Bernie Blake was the regulars. They've gone. Made off!"

"Left town? Why?"

"Nothing for them here but trouble, nobody to make out payrolls. No reason to stick."

"And the valet as well," I said. "Rats leaving the sinking ship?"

"Ha ha!"

"You stuck," I said.

"Stay with the *Oriana*," Croft said, and looked serious for the first time. "My duty, you know."

"Who's to make your payroll?"

"Somebody'll come through. The *Oriana* is worth fancy money to some bloke."

"I wonder if those two might be in the City just now," Bierce said, when Croft had taken his leave. "Did you get their names?"

"Jink Ratched and Bernie Blake."

"Of course they could have any names they chose by now," Bierce said. "And already signed aboard a ship bound for Australia."

"Who is the young fellow with the big hat?"

"Who indeed," Bierce said.

———

James Dix was a different matter, a stiff young man with a habit of turning his eyes but not his head, so that he looked even more suspicious than Croft, but he responded to Bierce in such a forthright style that it was impossible not to trust him.

Billings had finished a big book that he hoped to publish—photographs of Dix in a multitude of exercises and poses to show musculature in use. There were some twenty-six photographs of him and an equal amount of two young men in Baltimore, where Billings hailed from. The university there had been engaged to publish the book.

Billings had begun a similar female enterprise, employing Miss Powers, but had only fifteen or so photographs when Mr. Hearst put the kibosh to it. Billings had done all his own photography; he, Dix, had never taken a photograph. He was not interested in the craft. No, he had never visited aboard the *Oriana* except on the night of the murder, and couldn't think then why he had been invited.

"I suppose because there can never be too many eligible young men at a shipboard ball," Bierce said.

"I am not eligible," Dix snapped. "I am engaged to be married to Miss Eugenia Brookhurst of Stockton."

Bierce congratulated him.

Dix went on. "Billings was going to set up banks of cameras, so he could take photographs in a speedy—serial, I think he said—sequencing. That way if you had a method to run the photographs in the same serial way, it would be almost as though the figure was in motion. Mr. Hearst and Billings were both interested in making photographs in action, you see."

"Photographing you and Miss Powers?"

"Well, Mr. Hearst put a stop to him photographing Miss Powers. And he had to find some cash to buy his cameras with. The university back in Baltimore was maybe going to help him with that. And he was working on ways to print photographs in the newspaper. But of course it's all up now. You think he was coshed, don't you, Mr. Bierce?"

"I do," Bierce said.

"Coroner's just trying to calm things down, calling it an accident."

"Was Billings making a series of photographs of the Graces?" Bierce asked. "We found one of a pretty young lady seated on a column, labeled 'Aglaia.' The other two would be Euphrosyne and Thalia. The daughters of Eurynome."

Dix shook his head thoughtfully. "Might've been from Baltimore, when he was there making photographs. You know, he did say he had photographs of a young lady there he was proud of."

"Were unclothed young women his special interest? I cite what you have told us about Miss Powers."

Stiffening his posture, chin out, Dix said, "Jasper Billings was not like that!"

"You would not say that he was unsuitably attracted to Miss Powers?"

"No, I would not say that! He was engaged to the young woman in Baltimore of whom he spoke to me often!"

"It is very important to Mr. Hearst that the plates that were taken from the darkroom be found," Bierce said. "Did Billings have any theory as to who might have taken them?"

"He was in a panic Mr. Hearst would think he had made off with them himself!" Dix said.

After the session with James Dix, Bierce and I took a stroll along the waterfront. It was a brilliant day. We could see the glint of glass of the windows of Sea Point above us. The yacht fleet in the little harbor all pulled on their anchor lines in perfect parallels.

Bierce said, "If one asks enough questions, ultimately it may transpire that one asks the right one."

"Why was Billings murdered?"

"Because of the plates, but maybe not because of their theft."

———

"These British sea lords of Sausalito are surely an arrogant bunch," Bierce said when we were back at our table in the Bon Ton. "They must be second sons for the most part, swaggering around the town, cutting lesser mortals dead, with their infuriating sense of noblesse oblige toward San Francisco maidens."

"And here comes the one we are looking for," I said, gazing out the dirty window of the Bon Ton.

But Charles Peavine was also a different breed from Bierce's generality.

He indeed entered the Bon Ton with a swagger, a lean, broad-shouldered gent of perhaps thirty, clad in an officer's blue cap, a navy blue doublebreasted jacket, white flannels, a high collar, and striped cravat, very cock of the walk.

When we were seated he ordered a lager from the aproned barkeep and looked from Bierce to me with a supercilious eyebrow raised. He had a high-color face, a neat beak of a nose, a curly beard and moustache, and bronze hair so carefully brushed that I had a picture of him frowning at the mirror as he went at his scalp with twin brushes with silver monograms.

"Well, Mr. Bierce—and Mr. Redmond, is it?—what can I do for you?"

"We are interested in the murder of Captain Larkyn, sir. And especially in his photographic collection."

"Ah, Augie and his photographs. What can I say, gentlemen? He was a collector. That was his pride and his obsession."

"And his death," Bierce said.

"Ah, do you think so?" Peavine said. "I didn't know such a solution had been arrived at."

"Have you a better theory, sir?"

"I have no theory at all," Peavine said, smiling and spreading his hands wide.

"Tell us, who would wish him dead?" Bierce inquired.

Peavine shrugged with his hands.

"Larkyn was not a friend of yours?" I asked.

"I detested the old bag of cess. You will find that attitude common among the British of Sausalito."

"Because of his treatment of young women?" Bierce wanted to know.

"Because of his nasty nature."

"As a collector?"

Peavine sipped his lager and traced a thumbnail across the foam on his moustache. His eyes were sharp and cold. He did not respond.

"You are aware that Mr. Hearst's photographer was also murdered?" Bierce said.

"Yes, yes. Small town, this. Murder, was it?"

"And you know of Billings's projects, photographing nude men and women in action?"

"Yes, yes."

"And that Miss Powers had been photographed in a natural state?"

"Well known."

"The photographic plates of Miss Powers have disappeared from Billings's studio, and a photograph that may have been produced from one of them has turned up in Captain Larkyn's cabin."

"Is that so?" Peavine said, and looked suddenly interested. "By Jove!" he said.

"Do you draw any conclusions from that, sir?"

"The conclusion might be drawn that Augie Larkyn shared Miss Powers's charms with young Willie Hearst, but I would not, personally, draw it." He grinned at his cleverness.

"But you would not be surprised by such activity on the part of Miss Powers?"

"Well, I must say—yes, I would! She does not seem that sort of a young lady. Although one has made such misjudgments many times!"

Through the window a quartet of rust-colored lateen sails could be seen heading north beyond the anchored yachts. Peavine turned to follow my gaze.

"The fishing fleet," he said. "There's a colony of Portuguese up around the point, you know. Their big celebration of the Holy Ghost is coming up."

"Sausalito is known for its celebrations," Bierce said.

Peavine's imperial eyebrows rose again.

"For instance," Bierce continued, "mysterious occasions up in the hills behind the town, drumming, dancing, strong drink. Not the Holy Ghost exactly, but Bacchic revels, Dionysiac, maenads. I have heard your name connected with these affairs, Captain Peavine."

"So that is what this is all about," Peavine said, laughing.

"Was Larkyn involved?"

"Turned up once that I know of. Years ago."

"Photographs taken?"

"Ah, it would have been impossible. Bad light, you understand. Flickering flames of a bonfire, torchlight. By Jove, the most recent of those events was years ago! Can you believe it has anything to do with the present instance?"

Bierce said, "If you will allow me to speculate, Captain Peavine. Larkyn attended the event once in your recollection. You and he are not friends. Could this be because his activities at the affair offended the members of the revels?"

Peavine grinned winningly and said, "Bull's-eye, Mr. Bierce. August was a disgusting goat of a fellow. Odious. Offended one and all. These revels were not crude, you understand. The ladies were not wantons but Victorian ladies who liked to cast aside their pruderies from time to time. A number of widows among them."

"God's second noblest gift to mankind," Bierce said.

"Sir?"

Bierce repeated it. Peavine showed his curly-bearded grin. "And the noblest?"

Bierce shrugged it off, but I had heard his response on previous occasions in previous saloons: "Bad girls!"

"And you were the Master of the Revels?" Bierce said to Peavine.

"That is certainly more rank than I would give myself. Please do not request the ladies' names. My lips are sealed."

"Except for that of August Larkyn."

"Indeed."

I saw that Peavine was not going to obstruct, but would give no more assistance than what he was asked; and the whole panoply was so large I did not see how Bierce would get a grip on it. Still, I had come to like Charles Peavine as an honest man, and his arrogance appeared only a Sausalito uniform he donned on occasion.

Peavine said, "The whole business ended almost five years ago, gentlemen." He propped his fingertips together and gazed at Bierce over them.

"But meanwhile August Larkyn pursued his course, which proved ultimately suicidal."

"Which is not of particular interest to me," Peavine said. He rose, gracefully, and nodded to Bierce and me. "Good day, gentlemen."

Just then a small maritime figure stamped in from the sunny street outside, black-capped, black-suited, and booted, grizzle-bearded with a lean face and snapping black eyes, a powerful little man whose presence captured the eye.

"Good afternoon, Presidente," Peavine said.

"Good morning, good sir," the maritime gent said and clacked his heels together along with a military head-bow. Peavine made introductions. This was Captain Rudy Carvalho of the Sausalito Portuguese colony.

"President of this spring's Catholic Festival?" Bierce inquired.

"That is correct, gentlemen," Captain Carvalho said with a bow. "There will be music and dancing, and beauty, with Queen Isabel and her attendants."

"And these preparations are under way?" Bierce asked.

"They have been under way since the Festa of last year. A president is elected. I have the honor and misfortune to be that, sir."

He bowed and strolled off to a far corner of the bar, so straight-backed it was as though he was trying to make himself appear taller. He was greeted with respect by the three men seated at the bar.

"Captain?" Bierce said to Peavine in a low voice.

"He owns a squadron of fishing vessels. He is quite a fellow. He is responsible for the care and feeding of the Portuguese poor for this year. Fortunately there are not many of them. Some widows and orphans. The men are hardworking. They are Azorean for the most part."

We remained standing with him.

"He is a local hero," Peavine went on. "Last year a dead whale washed up on the beach in the middle of Portuguese-town over there," he nodded to the west. "Terrible stink. Terrible pother. Meetings. Protests. Wailing and gnashing. My Lord, you would have thought El Draque had landed! What did Rudy do? He arranged for the dead beast to be towed out to the Farallons and blown up with some sticks of dynamite.

"And now, Mr. Bierce, Mr. Redmond—" Peavine donned his own naval cap, and sauntered off outside into the street.

Bierce and I embarked on the afternoon ferry back to the City.

I was thinking of the photograph that must not be of Eliza Lindley.

"You are very quiet, Tom," Bierce said.

"Thinking bad thoughts," I said.

CHAPTER SEVEN

INTIMACY, n. A relation into which fools are providentially drawn for their mutual destruction.
> — *The Devil's Dictionary*

WEDNESDAY, MAY 12, 1891

The first of the Annie Laurie pieces had appeared in the previous Friday's *Examiner*. Winifred Sweet had accompanied Eliza and a Chinese child to city court that week.

LITTLE LIN CHOW

SHE WAS INDUCED TO PREVARICATE ABOUT HER BETTER HALF

IDENTITY OF NOT MUCH ACCOUNT

The clever tactics of attorney Duggan and Miss Lindley of the Presbyterian Stockton Street Mission in besting the Mongol slavers

The white-bearded, noble-domed judge gazes down from his high perch on the tiny, frail Chinese girl summoned in terror before the bench.

Lin Chow is beset by men of two races, one of them attorney Duggan, who is trying to free her from her cruel bondage, the other a Mongol master, represented here by his white attorney. Last month the child was removed from a disgusting brothel on Grant Avenue by Federal officers and taken to the Stockton Street Mission, but now the arrogant Celestial brazenly claims she was the bride of a friend and demands her return.

Miss Lindley, Directrix of the Mission, wears black-rimmed spectacles. Without them she has a sweet pale-complexioned face; with them she looks New-Englander severe and uncompromising, which is how she is now, gazing on the proceedings from her seat behind little Lin Chow. Attorney Duggan is pursuing Lin Chow's freedom on her behalf, waggling a long finger to emphasize his words.

The clever slave masters have devised a plan to get her away from the Christian influence of the Mission. Lew Wing Fong presents himself as the representative of the true husband of little Lin Chow, and demands to be allowed to take this "wife" to her husband. He is unable to produce proper assurances of her marriage, but he fixes her with a stern and monitory gaze as the judge inquires if she wishes to return to her "husband."

The terrified child squeaks reluctantly that she does.

Miss Lindley and attorney Duggan confer on this matter, and arrive at a clever strategy. A Chinese convert who has been in the Mission is induced to impersonate the missing "husband."

"Is this your husband, child?" Judge Tallent inquires, leaning down from his judicial roost.

"Oh, yes!" the confused and frightened child replies, and rushes to grasp her "husband"'s arm.

"Are you certain that this is your proper husband?" the judge persists.

"Oh, yes!" the child insists. "We were married in China by the Three Writings and the Six Ceremonies."

"Dismissed!" Judge Tallent calls out, and cracks his gavel down.

So are the cruel slavers confounded and Attorney Duggan triumphant, and the no longer unfortunate child is borne off to the Stockton Street Mission by the kindly hand of Miss Lindley.

ANNIE LAURIE

Eliza seemed gratified with what Miss Sweet had written, and she was sure the Mission's directors would be pleased as well.

I took her to supper, not in Chinatown, of which I had become leery, for myself and for her, but to the Old Poodle Dog, where it no doubt occurred to me that attentions of the maitre d' would impress her with my worth. We dined on clams in shell, clear soup, crab cutlets, asparagus with Hollandaise, then small valentines of steaks glorious to behold, nestled beside glistening broiled quail on a bed of toast with slivers of fried potato; burgundy with this course, a chilled sauterne with the pineapple sherbet, coffee after.

We talked of everything and nothing, and Eliza was pretty and soft and appreciative, and not the implacable heroine who rather disturbed me. Our histories matched remarkably and sadly, for she was a widow with a child who had perished from typhoid at the age of two, while my own wife had died of grief after a stillbirth. After supper I asked her to come to my rooms and sample some champagne, and she assented, although she was silent on our walk to Sacramento Street. In my rooms we sipped champagne and the evening's event seemed to slow and stretch with a kind of heavy inevitability.

I had reason to surmise that Eliza Lindley was not entirely the saint Father Flanagan had termed her. When she said that she must return to her quarters at the Mission, I said, "Don't go."

She stood before the door with her wrap in her hands, turning, her eyes a flash of blue meeting mine. "Is that what you want, Tom?"

"It is what I want very much."

She hung her wrap back on the rack.

I took her home about eleven.

THURSDAY, MAY 13, 1891

In the morning I found Winnie Sweet with Bierce in his office. With one hip propped on a corner of Bierce's desk beside his pet skull, Winnie wore a lacy white blouse and a necklace of red stones. Sunlight slashing through the window turned to fire in her hair. Bierce leaned back in his chair with hands locked behind his head, looking pleased with himself.

I congratulated Miss Sweet on her piece on little Lin Chow.

"Thank you, Tom!"

"Winnie and I were talking about the arrangement at Sea Point," Bierce said. "I approve of it, for there is no master, no mistress, and consequently no slaves. As you know, I have come to regard the marriage contract as one of mutual slavery."

"What a grand and toplofty attitudinarianism!" Winnie exclaimed, fingering the eyehole of the skull. "Isn't he the nonpareil, Tom?"

Bierce was not to be interrupted. "We were speaking of Sea Point, where Miss Powers may possess an ultimate freedom but pursues an immediate enslavement, while Willie worries about his lady consort more than a man of his responsibilities has the time for."

"I like Miss Powers just fine!" Winnie said. "She may be a fallen woman, but she is a very charming young person. Our Willie is lucky to have her."

Bierce was still thinking about Tessie when Winnie Sweet took her leave, a sharp rap of heels diminishing in the hallway.

"Of course Tessie would be even more vulnerable if she were his wife."

"The photographs?"

He squinted at the sun beaming through the window. "It is as though some past—the region of sobs—pursues her."

"A male past?"

"The maintenance of secrets is the glory of the gender," Bierce said pompously.

We spoke of Miss Powers's provenance.

"I understand that she was a waitress in a saloon at Harvard when Willie was a student there," Bierce said. He sighed and said, "A woman has secrets in her past as she has face powder in her reticule."

It was easy to become impatient with his trying out clever sentences for "Prattle" on me.

"What of the missing photographic plates?"

"It is possible that they have been destroyed."

"By whom?"

"By someone of a moral bent."

———

I left the Examiner Building and was heading for the Stockton Street Mission when a tall man came up beside me on Kearny Street, and something hard prodded my ribs.

"Sonny Bill wants to see you," he said.

Sonny Bill was the master of the Sam Yup tong, and thus, in fact, of all Chinatown. It was known that he employed white bodyguards, and this man was white, clean-shaven, hat pulled down on his forehead, and one hand invisible where he held the revolver in his pocket with its muzzle nudging me in the side.

When I inquired what this was about, he didn't reply. I thought it must be Annie Laurie's piece in today's *Examiner*.

We turned toward the bay on Stockton; the street changed into a foreign country of red-and-gold banners, wind-dried ducks gibbeted in shopwindows, piercing smells, Chinese in conical hats hurrying past us, men in black pajamas with loaded shoulder-poles, one woman hobbling on crippled feet, no notice taken of me or my companion. Chinese restaurants, some of them three stories high, exhaled cooking smells; in an alley off to the right cribbed girls leaned out their windows shrilling invitations; a little farther along women had braced cooking pots over a little fire, and a pigtailed fellow displayed a rack of cigars.

Our goal was an open-air barbershop, three steps above the sidewalk, where crowds of Chinese men waited on either side observing their chief, who was seated in a barber's chair with a lathered face and the barber leaning over him. My captor thrust me forward between the ranks of Chinese giving way before us.

With half his face lathered, the other clean-shaven, Sonny Bill sat upright to greet me. Behind him was another tall white bodyguard, squinting at me out of a hard face. Spectators whispered behind me. The barber stood back, razor in one hand, towel in the other.

"So, Mister Redmon', you have come see Sonny Bill!" Sonny Bill said.

"Yes, I have," I said, detaching my arm from the bodyguard's grip.

"So, Mister Redmon', you become friendly with Missy Ling-ling of Stockton Street Mission."

"That is correct."

"Missy Lingling live danger life in Chinatown," Sonny Bill said.

I didn't respond to that.

"So, Mister Redmon', you write newspape' story China sing-song girl?"

I shrugged.

"You no write more?" Sonny Bill said.

I thought about that, and about Annie Laurie, and it seemed I could shake my head.

"You no write more newspape' story, that is correct?"

I shrugged, pretending an ease I did not feel. "Not just now, that is correct."

"You write more, very danger for Missy Lingling."

"Is that so?"

"That is so, Mister Redmon'. Very danger for white lady in Chinatown, very slip places, hole in street for fall down, rot wood place in bad house. Crazee peoples."

"I see," I said.

The lather on the right side of his face was drying in a scurf of white pimples. He swiped at his cheek with the back of his hand. He looked surprisingly young, with black eyes sharp as gimlets.

"So you see, Mister Redmon', danger in Chinatown for Missy Lingling, but can be more danger also. And you also, Mister Redmon'!"

It seemed to be the end of the interview, for he sank back in the barber chair and the barber stepped forward to lean over him. I retreated past my captor, who seemed to have finished his duties with me, for he had faded away from my side.

A tall fellow in a black dress and a black flat-brimmed hat crowded past me. There was another with him, dressed the same, two tall Chinese men holding up revolvers like gifts to be presented. The bodyguards had their hands raised as though reaching for something on a high shelf. There was absolute silence. One of the highbinders took a quick step forward to jam the muzzle of his revolver into Sonny Bill's face. With a pop like a dropped melon, blood slashed over the barber's white apron and the framed mirror behind him.

The two highbinders stood swinging their revolvers around at the crowd, which had magically diminished. I didn't know what to do with my hands. Quick as a dance team the two descended the steps and were gone.

With this, the Feng Yups replaced the Sam Yups as masters of Chinatown, and I broke my promise to Sonny Bill and wrote a gee-whiz front-page story about his assassination, to be rewritten by Sam Chamberlain in stronger anti-Chinese terms.

CHAPTER EIGHT

*ORPHAN, n. A living person whom death has deprived of the power of
filial ingratitude—a privation appealing with a particular eloquence to
all that is sympathetic in human nature.*
—The Devil's Dictionary

SUNDAY, MAY 16, 1891

In the hills above Sausalito, our little procession followed its
leader on this Sunday outing, Miss Eliza Lindley striding
ahead, manzanita switch in hand with which she indicated the
trail. Following her were some eleven Chinese maidens, ages
maybe eight to twelve, with the translator Fah Loo in the midst
of them, and bringing up the rear were plump Miss Cochran,
the English teacher, carrying a Chinese-decorated water bottle
in a kind of leather harness, and yours truly Thomas Redmond,
Miss Lindley's lover and servant, with the picnic basket.

We had come across on the ferry, past the Union Jack yachts
in the anchorage, with the children plastered along the rail
pointing and jabbering; we disembarked and filed along the
Sausalito streets until Eliza found the trail she was looking for.
We wound uphill through manzanita brush and live oaks,
with the view of the bay spreading out more and more widely
beneath us at every curve of the trail.

Sometimes the littlest girl would take Eliza's hand, skipping along beside her, and the second littlest Fah Loo's. The others kept their pace close to one another. Miss Cochran furnished water to sweaty little faces crowned with black hair.

At last we halted on a grassy patch beneath an oak; the girls crowded around Eliza, who beckoned me over with the basket. Black eyes gazed at me out of blank little faces. Most wore their hair in braids and spotless pajama suits in white and pastels. Eliza's pink cheeks were bright with perspiration.

She and Fah Loo spread out the tablecloth while the girls began a laughing game of slapping hands and spinning, hair braids flying. Eliza and I sat together, joined by Miss Cochran.

"It is a comprehensive view," I said. San Francisco's hills were on the right, the Coast Range foothills extending away to the upper reaches of the bay on the left. The bay was spotted with ships and scows, scarves of smoke drifting eastward. The girls had stopped their game and were tightly grouped again, one of them pointing. Fah Loo joined them.

"What is it?" Eliza said, rising quickly.

Fah Loo only rolled her eyes at her. Their attention was fixed upon a particular two-masted rusty steamer beyond the island of Alcatraz, stationary and showing no smoke.

The sight of the steamer had spoiled the children's mood. And I realized what it was, without Eliza having to tell me.

"It is the *Oliver Ferris,*" Miss Cochran said.

With broad arm gestures and a smiling face, Eliza seated the girls on the margins of the tablecloth. Fah Loo started a song in her small high voice:

Ring around a rosie
Pocketful of posies
Ashes— Ashes—

The girls began shrilling the words, two or three at first, the rest joining in, then Miss Cochran, Eliza, and I joining in.

A deeper voice joined in.

I switched around to see a khaki-clad figure leaning on a walking stick. He had bare knees, a many-pocketed jacket, a jaunty hat sporting a feather in the band, a curly fair beard. It was the yachtsman Charles Peavine, whom Bierce and I had met at the Bon Ton Saloon.

I rose to greet him and to explain this gathering. The little girls stared at him with their solemn faces. I introduced Eliza, Miss Cochran, and Fah Loo.

"Greetings, ladies and Mr. Redmond!" Peavine said, smiling. "Welcome to the broad views of these grand old headlands."

It was in these grand old headlands that Peavine had presided as Master of the Revels.

"Will you share a sandwich with us, Captain Peavine?" Eliza said. "We have plenty, sir."

"Can't think of a single reason why not," Peavine said, "in this company of lovelies." He seated himself between Eliza and Fah Loo, bare knees gleaming palely in the sunlight.

"And these are the orphans of the Stockton Street Mission?" he said, smiling right and left.

"Indeed, sir, orphans, or saved souls, as you may call them also," Miss Cochran said.

"Aha!" Peavine said. "And this certainly must be the courageous lady Miss Lindley recently celebrated in the *Examiner* newspaper?"

Eliza's face turned pink.

"And there off Alcatraz is the ship that brought some of these children to San Francisco," Miss Cochran said, waving an arm.

"Ah!"

"Baled and barreled like so many anchovies," Miss Cochran continued in her always-indignant voice.

Peavine had raised himself to peer out at the bay. "The *Oliver Ferris!*" he said. "That rusty tub of corruption. The evil old gent has shuffled off but I hear that the son has roused himself to action. What's his name? Stone?"

"Frank Stone," Eliza said.

"Understand it is a hell ship for its crew, not to speak of the cargo," Peavine said. "Lying off like that because the crew's all vanished. The ship is so defective no one even wants to venture on it out of the Gate. D'you think young Frank Stone intends to continue his father's transportation schemes?"

"I don't know," Eliza said.

"Ah, but you know him, do you, Miss Lindley?"

She nodded, tight-lipped, and began distributing the half-sandwiches to the extended brown and pale little hands.

The children stuffed bread and chicken into their mouths as though this might be their last supper. Peavine was jovial company, conversing with Fah Loo, who was very pretty and shyly returned his attentions, and with Eliza and Miss Cochran. After lunch he joined with gusto in the grand game of all-fall-down amid the giggling, shrieking children. He was indeed a practiced hand at revels.

He brought the subject up himself: "In the old days I used to come up here with a group on full-moon nights, tootling and drumming and dancing. Down that way a bit," he said, flapping a broad hand toward the ravine to the north of our ridge. He winked at me as though we shared the secret.

"Captain Peavine is a British yachtsman," I said. "One of a number of such gentlemen in Sausalito."

"A yachtsman but not a gentleman, alas," he said with his

curly-bearded grin. "My father was a brewer, not a duke. Thus it is not necessary for me to be such a scoundrel."

"Such as Captain Larkyn," I said. Eliza was instantly attentive.

"Such as the dear departed," Peavine agreed, smiling.

"My countrymen are concerned that his murder may be an outbreak of class or national conflict," he said to me. "They refer to the Portuguese as wogs and wonder that the wogs resent them."

The little girls gazed at him with incomprehension as he spoke.

"The Portuguese have many reasons to resent them," Eliza said. "Among them the honor of their daughters."

I recalled the beautiful young queen of the Holy Ghost Festival whom Eliza and I had encountered on the dock after Larkyn's murder.

"I'm afraid that gathering the scalps of the natives is a custom of the country," Peavine said, and frowned as though he wished he had not said that.

"Ladies and Mr. Redmond, enjoy your outing!" he said, rising. "I am determined to conquer this noble hillside."

He thanked Eliza for the sustenance, saluted the children, and left us, striding on up the trail, stabbing the ground with his walking stick.

"What a charming person," Eliza said. "How do you know him, Tom?"

"Bierce and I questioned him about the murder of Captain Larkyn."

Fah Loo chirped, "Very nice man with shiny knees!" She loved Eliza with all her heart. Several Chinese men with proper credentials had applied for her hand in marriage, as they must for any planned nuptials with the girls trained in the housekeeping arts by the Mission, but Fah Loo had refused her suitors to remain with Eliza.

"Has your friend Mr. Bierce come to any conclusions about the crime?" Eliza asked, folding napkins back into the picnic basket.

"He has not."

I had determined never to mention to her the fact that one of the photographs in Captain Larkyn's collection had been her likeness.

The children clustered around Miss Cochran, who was holding up a printed placard and shaking a finger. "Little!" she said.

"Litto!" the girls shrilled in chorus.

When the sun had quartered across the sky we trooped back down the ridge into Sausalito for the four o'clock ferry, which docked at the railroad pier. In our single file along the main street sidewalk I had a glimpse of Tessie Powers, slim in a bright dress, with bonneted curls, turning in to the dry-goods store. And we were passed by a swift-moving buggy in which the presidente of the Portuguese Holy Ghost celebration, Captain Carvalho, neat-bearded in his nautical cap, was seated beside an attractive, dark-eyed young woman with a parasol.

Sausalito was proving itself a very small town.

———

That night I woke with that clutch of desperation of not knowing where I was. A window was a rectangular pale shape halved by a crossbar; my closet door, with its hook from which clothing hung, was the shape of a menacing man—my own room! There were muted sounds, Eliza murmuring in her sleep; she was praying. Praying for forgiveness for fornication with Thomas Redmond?

I resented her Protestant prayers. Her voice ceased when I hissed her name.

The pale oblong of her face rose above mine. "I was seeking guidance, Tom," she whispered.

"About us?"

"No."

"What, then?"

"I have a life other than you," she said. "I had a life before you."

I had been careful to avoid demanding to know more of her life before me because I did not, yet, wish to counter with confidences of my own.

She had been briefly married to a young fellow in Massachusetts who had died in a railway accident. In San Francisco she had found the Stockton Street Mission, or it had found her. She possessed a lovely bosom and hips fashioned for childbearing. But her refugee children were her children.

"Your life before me?" I said.

"It has come back. Someone I knew in Cambridge. Here in San Francisco."

Frank Stone, by name. The owner of the slave ship *Oliver Ferris* that we had seen that day off Alcatraz. The rise of jealousy was like something foreign swelling in my chest.

"Were you in love with him?"

"I was besotted with him. When I came West I had thought to join him here, but he had mysteriously disappeared. In that time I found my Savior, and the Mission. And was saved. And have found you. But now he is here."

"Does he want you back?"

"Yes," she whispered.

"And you?"

"No. He is a devil, Tom. The night that Captain Larkyn was murdered aboard the *Oriana,* the night I asked you to escort me, I thought he might be there."

"He was a friend of Larkyn's?"

"His father was."

Peavine had spoken of the father. I put an arm around her solidity and warmth and held her against me. I could feel her breath on my cheek as she whispered, "As Captain Peavine suggested, I think he intends to follow his father's trade."

"It is interesting to me that it is *against* his father's trade that you—do what you do."

"Or it is because of what I do that he will follow his father's trade."

"He hates you, then?"

"Loves or hates. I don't think he knows the difference. But he may have to prove he can have me back. He has come twice now. And not only that. This *Examiner* series with Annie Laurie—your piece on the assassination of Sonny Bill—" Her breath on my cheek again, she whispered, "You must be careful of him. He has highbinders who are his guards and enforcers."

"Chinese?"

"He is in league with the Feng Yups. He had gone away when the Sam Yups were in power. He is a friend of the Feng Yups, as his father was."

"In the import trade?"

"I think not yet."

I whistled. "I'll take you away from all this, Eliza."

"No."

"How can I leave you here without some—protection?"

She stirred and moved her head so that the soft mass of her hair traversed my chest. "It may be you who will need protection—if we are to—go on. And if he knows you are writing those news pieces for Miss Sweet."

That was worth a trickle of fear up the back of my neck.

"Because of *me*!" Eliza said.

CHAPTER NINE

PANDEMONIUM, n. Literally, the Place of All the Demons. Most of them have escaped into politics and finance, and the place is now used as a lecture hall by the Audible Reformer. When disturbed by his voice the ancient echoes clamor appropriate responses most gratifying to his pride of distinction.

— *The Devil's Dictionary*

TUESDAY, MAY 18, 1891

I sat across a table from my father, the gent, at Malvolio's for our monthly dinner together. He worked for the Southern Pacific Railroad, passing out funds in the legislature to keep legislators voting the way Collis P. Huntington desired. As my mother said of him, he was an expert at giving away money long before he began to be paid for it.

His hair had gone white at the temples, and his beard was striped with white in a somewhat skunklike effect; his napkin was tucked into his collar and he went after his tagliarini with utensils in both hands. His approach was that everything that occurred in San Francisco and environs was well known in the state governmental circles in Sacramento, and he usually saved whatever gem of gossip or plain information he had garnered for the second course of an expensive Italian dinner.

"Young William Randolph Hearst," he said. "Your employer."

"He is that."

"Daddy George Hearst," he said. "The Indians had a name for him, 'Talks to the earth,' or some such. An eye for mineral, or an ear, I guess. The Ophir mine! The Homestake! Went back to Missouri a rich man and married a sweet little schoolteacher half his age, Phoebe Apperson. Gave her one son to dote on, Willie Hearst. Senator Hearst turned over the *Examiner* to his son to play with. Called him Buster Boy."

I wondered what he was getting at. "The senator died in February," I said.

"Leaving all the beeswax to the little lady, yes," my father said, nodding. "Well, Buster Boy had him a nanny name of Emma Cowan. Worshipped Mrs. Hearst, loved her charge. Lives in Sacramento now, not half a block from your mother."

Aha.

"Seems she was down here in the evil City last week or so, visited Mrs. Hearst in her palace out on Russian Hill. Buster Boy has a lady friend that lives with him over in Sausalito, no benefit of matrimony. Now: Emma Cowan happened to see what she thought was a shocking naughty photograph like a French postcard. Just happened to see it, she said, which I guess means Mrs. Hearst didn't show it to her, and maybe means more than that. Anyhow, she saw it.

"Now, it seems Emma Cowan had also visited Willie Hearst and met his lady friend."

"And the photograph was of her."

"Naked as a snake," the gent said, nodding again.

It was tiring to think of explaining the nude photographs of Tessie Powers to my father.

"Along with her a tall young fellow just as naked and front

on, if you understand me. She was holding up a kind of box thing as though presenting it to him. Emma was fair shocked."

So was I. The photograph of Tessie Powers I had seen in Captain Larkyn's collection came to mind's eye, and then the thought that by some photographic trickery the man, who must be James Dix, had been added. For what purpose? To shock Mrs. Hearst as it had shocked Emma Cowan? For money, or leverage?

"I wonder what it means," I said.

"I've been wondering that myself, son," he said, leaning back as the pasta plates were cleared away. "Blackmail, d'you suppose?"

"To show Willie Hearst to bust up his romance? That won't work."

My father pulled a face.

"It happens I know of some photographs of Tessie Powers," I said, and explained. "I wonder if naked James Dix could have been added to make an innocent photograph something else."

"Do admire modern magic," my father said. He brushed his hands together in anticipation as a plate of scallopini was placed before him.

"I don't expect Emma would have been able to tell that," he added. "Nor Mrs. Hearst."

If she hadn't had the photograph fabricated herself. If it *had* been fabricated. I pondered whether to bring the subject of Bierce into the conversation. My father disapproved of Bierce because of Bierce's disapprovals. I had argued with him that there were many things worthy of disapproval, and he had pointed out that if you disapproved of something a ton that was only worth a hundredweight's disapproval, then you had disapproved too much.

"In fact," I said, "Mrs. Hearst has asked Bierce to do what he can to help her stave off scandal as far as Willie is concerned."

My father gazed reflectively at his plate, and adjusted its position by a half an inch.

"Willie Hearst has never tried to hide his relation with Tessie Powers," I said. "But the photographic plates were stolen, and someone has access to developing prints from them."

So I had to inform him of the murder and the investigation to date. Usually he did most of the talking.

"No idea who has those plates now?"

"Larkyn had one developed print. We didn't find the plates."

Making interested sounds, my father dug into his segundo piatti.

"Sausalito's a queer place," I said. "There's a Portuguese town, New Town, and Old Town with a colony of snooty English: the yachting set, who are a fairly wild bunch, and more sedate English gentry."

"You say this fellow Billings was taking pictures of ladies with no clothes on. To show their muscles? Queer kind of thing to be interested in, i'n't it? Females' *muscles*?"

"You remember a photographer named Muybridge who took photographs of Leland Stanford's trotting horse in action—to settle a bet whether a horse's four hoofs were off the ground in a gallop?"

"Won the bet, too," he said nodding.

"If you run those photographs fast one after another you just about have the image in motion," I said.

"Muybridge shot the feller seduced his wife, you know. Jury let him off, too. English gent."

"One-eyed jacks," I said, and my father blushed for my language.

He mopped at his beard with the lap end of his napkin. "Speaking of nautical events," he said, "it seems you hopped off an SP ferry boat to see how long it took to rescue you. Took most of the working day, as I recall."

"It just seemed that long. I'm sorry if it embarrassed you."

He shrugged and said, "Part and parcel with an offspring working for the *Examiner,* I guess. There's other newspapers than Willie Hearst's, my boy."

"They don't pay as well," I said.

"That is a consideration," he said, sighing. "Another matter, my boy. Your mother hears you've taken up with a young lady down here. Wants to know if she's a good Catholic girl. You know, she does rattle on about wanting that grandson!"

"I'm afraid Miss Lindley is a Protestant. She's director of the Stockton Street Mission."

He was nodding as though he already knew that. "Serious intent?"

I remembered Father Flanagan mentioning that he thought the True Faith was somewhere in Eliza's background. She had never mentioned it to me. I nodded.

"Just don't break your mother's heart."

He had broken my mother's heart so many times it must consist entirely of fracture lines. He stretched to take from his coat pocket a sheet of folded newsprint, which he unfolded and presented to me.

It was from this morning's *Examiner.* Many of the words were my own, Winifred Sweet having furbished my language to some effect:

A SOUL ON THE LINE

A NEW ENGLAND LADY TO THE RESCUE

INVASION OF THE CITY OF PEKIN

The strategies of Miss Lindley of the
Stockton Street Mission, and the fulminations of
frustrated highbinders

A note of crude misspellings describing brutalities and injustices to touch the hardest of hearts was delivered to Miss Eliza Lindley, the indomitable Directrix of the Stockton Street Mission. If she would come at four o'clock to a certain Chinatown address a soul might be saved. Miss Lindley recognized the address as that of the City of Pekin, a notorious stew where Mongol tong men lived on the earnings of slave girls cruelly imprisoned and forced into a life of hideous degradation and servitude. A wisp of blue cloth had been sent as a token of recognition, and the note indicated that the child would be at the door at the appointed time.

There was no time to call for Patrolman Perkin, her usual guardian and strong right arm, but the courageous Miss Lindley summoned her translator Fah Loo to her side, and set off at a fast pace for the appointment.

The door was opened by a grim-faced female. Behind her cowered the girl child, holding up a wisp of blue cloth, then fleeing Miss Lindley with her silk sahm fluttering behind her. The captive girls must pretend they had made no attempt to contact the Mission, or they will be horribly punished. Fah Loo and Miss Lindley hastened after their quarry and captured the terrified child.

They were deep into one of San Francisco's most dangerous fleshpots without police protection and the doorkeeper shrieking an alarm. The girls are worth hundreds, even thousands, of dollars to their Mongol masters. Miss Lindley and Fah Loo fled back down the hallway, each holding a hand of the sobbing child. Men shouted after them. They burst out onto the street. Just outside was a group of tourists viewing Chinatown under the stewardship of Mr. Fenton, a photographer friend of Miss Lindley's. The three instantly mingled with the group, while a menacing trio of high-binders with scowling Asiatic faces and concealed revolvers stood helplessly by muttering threats.

The weeping rescued girl clung to Miss Lindley's hand as she was escorted to safety in the midst of the surprised and pleased group of tourists.

At the Mission she will be taught English and homemaking arts in a group of children like herself, by instructors whose goal it is to make up by love and understanding for the miseries these rescued captives had endured.

ANNIE LAURIE

"Miss Lindley is the young woman who has inflamed my heart," I said.

"She sounds a rare one," my father said. "Too bad she's a prot." He looked at me anxiously.

"Your mother wants that grandson, but don't break her heart," he said again.

"Easy enough to join the Church," I said, and the words seemed to reverberate in my skull as the waiter leaned over the table to inquire if we wished spumoni.

CHAPTER TEN

INDISCRETION, n. The guilt of woman.
— The Devil's Dictionary

THURSDAY, MAY 20, 1891

With Eliza in her office at the Mission was a young woman with skin as softly white as chrysanthemums, and dark eyes that took me in quickly as I entered. She had removed her bonnet and her hair was black and lustrous, done up in a bun at the back of her small neat head. She sat on one side of Eliza's desk, Eliza on the other.

She was Miss da Costa—Isabella, as Eliza called her. I recalled her from the wharf the night of August Larkyn's murder. She was quite beautiful.

"Isabella will be the queen of next month's Holy Ghost festival in Sausalito," Eliza said.

"I have met Captain Carvalho," I said.

"The presidente," Miss da Costa said, nodding. "He is a very fine man, Mr. Redmond. He is responsible for this so-important event, which I face with dread."

"Isabella is a reluctant queen," Eliza said.

Miss da Costa flipped white hands up on either side of her pretty face. "There are so many things that bind a girl to her destiny, and a life she may not desire," she said.

"You don't wish to remain in the Portuguese colony of Sausalito?"

"There is a larger world than Sausalito."

"Isabella has a beautiful soprano voice," Eliza said. "She wishes for a career as a singer."

"I am a dancer also," Miss da Costa said; she did not seem to lack self-confidence. I saw that she both pleased and amused Eliza.

I suggested that her selection as the festival queen might be a step toward such a career.

"It is not!" she said, with a grimace. "It is a step toward a career as a fisherman's wife!"

"Is that such a terrible career, my dear?" Eliza said gently.

"And motherhood of ten children! Do you think, Miss Lindley, that there is then time for singing and dancing?"

She made a motion with her shoulders, as though pressing against confining bonds.

I said, "I understand that Captain Carvalho in his position is charged with providing for the poor and unfortunates of his district."

"Yes, sir, he is. But he can call on the other important gentlemen to assist him in this. All must provide the assistance he requires. You are interested in the Portuguese of Sausalito, Mr. Redmond?"

"Mr. Redmond and his friend Mr. Bierce are investigating the murder of Captain Larkyn," Eliza said.

Miss da Costa's shoulder motion ceased and she became perfectly still. "That bad man," she said.

"You knew him, Miss da Costa?"

"Everyone in Sausalito knew him. How he swaggered when he walked along the street. How he showed his teeth when he encountered young women, as though he would devour them!" Her cheeks twitched in a mechanical smile.

But her face was shadowed with something that was not entirely distaste at the mention of Captain Larkyn.

"The British colony of Sausalito has several such swaggerers," I said.

"Oh, yes," Miss da Costa said, and pulled a long face. "Captain Bastable. Captain Jones."

"Are there young Englishmen interested in Portuguese young women?"

"Not to marry them," Miss da Costa said, chin up. "I prefer to meet the young Americans of San Francisco!"

I didn't know whether I was supposed to take this as a compliment or not. Eliza smiled at me, so perhaps I was.

"I have met Captain Peavine," I said.

"He is a nice English!"

"We were told that years ago he was a kind of director of events of some people dancing and carousing in the hills behind Sausalito."

It was a pretty sight when Miss da Costa colored, as though a pink shadow swept up her cheeks. "Oh, those old days," she said. "A young woman disappeared! A Portuguese young woman, who was to be a queen of the Festa like me!"

"Disappeared at the revels?"

"No, no, Mr. Redmond, not then. But there was rumor that she had been at the revels, and met there the kind of Englishman I have described. And disappeared. Her name was Flora Rodrigues."

"Murdered, you think, Isabella?" Eliza asked.

"That is what many think. There are others who like to think she ran away with her lover and has never returned."

"To marry a fisherman and mother ten children," I said. Eliza frowned at me. "Who was the lover?" I asked.

Miss da Costa raised her spread hands with a shrug. She had

very expressive shoulders, and a pretty pale neck girdled with a silver chain.

"An Englishman?"

"Ah, Mr. Redmond, I was very young then. I only know what others gossip, and they gossip every which way. Yes, maybe an Englishman. You must ask the good Captain Peavine."

"Who is not like the other Englishmen?"

"No, sir, he does not swagger so."

"He has told us the other English do not approve of him because he is not of aristocratic stock. Nor do they approve of Miss Powers," I added.

Miss da Costa colored again, not so spectacularly. Eliza was leaning on her elbows, watching her. Upstairs was the cheerful sound of rescued Chinese children at play.

"My mother says we must never speak of Miss Powers," Miss da Costa said.

I was certain that she was the veiled Moroccan dancer from Captain Larkyn's photographic collection who had moved seductively before the American flag when Bierce had riffled the photographs.

When she had taken her leave, I said to Eliza, "Miss da Costa was more involved with Captain Larkyn than she would like you, or me, to believe."

"Yes, she has learned lying as well as singing and dancing," Eliza said. "But no doubt she thought her very life was at stake. I love her anyhow."

I asked how they had come to know each other.

"The local priest in New Town Sausalito is very strict. I suppose I am her spiritual advisor."

"I remember we encountered her on the dock at Sausalito after the murder. She had decided to attend the ball despite your warnings about Larkyn."

Eliza looked down. The part of her hair was as precise as though drawn with a ruler. "I forgive her," she said. "I know well enough what it is to rebel against the restraints life has laid upon one."

"Larkyn had her photographs."

"Are they very—bad?"

"Not very bad," I said, to her relief. "But I believe you were right that she was in danger."

"Yes."

Larkyn had also possessed a not-very-bad one of Eliza.

———

These days Winnie Sweet was often to be found in Bierce's office. I did not think it was his desk skull that attracted her. I also thought that his competitive spirit might be involved, since she was considered Sam Chamberlain's discovery and terrain.

Her pose was familiar, a hip leaned against his desk and one foot in a shiny black boot extended as though she had been admiring it. She wore her usual blazing white blouse, her face high-colored and smiling.

She called out when she saw me look into the office. "Come on in, Tom! I've been listening to the Grand Panjandrum. He is pointing out the necessity for me to change my opinion about simply everything!" And she laughed gaily.

Bierce looked smugly severe.

"What opinion in particular, may I ask?" I asked.

"Oh, of Little Jim," she replied. "Do you know of Little Jim, Tom?"

I didn't.

"He's a street boy, with a crippled leg and a crutch. He's an orphan, or anyway he doesn't know who his parents are; born in jail, he thinks. He has the sweetest smile. He sits on the curbing there on Market, across from the Palace Hotel. People give him money, bits of food. He is so sweetly grateful, though he doesn't beg. I've talked to Doctor Jenks about him. Doctor Jenks thinks his leg might be repaired, though it would take a number of operations, and months in the hospital. But it could be done. I was going to do a piece on him, but Ambrose thinks I am a silly and sentimental woman."

"Leave be God's botchwork world," I said.

"That is exactly what he says! That I am silly and sentimental!" Winnie stepped away from the desk and, I thought, posed herself against the window where the sun made her hair gleam. She beamed down at Bierce who watched her admiringly.

"But I am *supposed* to be silly and sentimental!"

"And a woman," Bierce put in.

"And I would rather be sillily sentimental than cynically so, as you would have me."

"The *Examiner* likes you just the way you are!" Bierce said. "There!"

"But I don't think that *is* the way you are. You are a very intelligent young woman."

"Such a flatterer!" Winnie said, and smiled at me.

"The hardest thing it is to be," Bierce said, "is yourself. Because first of all you must discover what that is. That is hard work, my dear."

"Just when I thought I was a successful journalist," Winnie said. "The Chinatown pieces have gone well, don't you think, Tom?"

"Very well."

"*There* is a person who knows what she consists of. Miss Lindley. I have the greatest admiration for her."

I could only agree, although I was not sure that Eliza knew

exactly what she consisted of. I knew her in several guises, and suspected there were more. And loved her for all that and despite all that. Women had secrets just as they had face powder in their reticules, as Bierce had put it. And the past was the region of sobs.

"Sam will find a way for me to interview the president and Mrs. Harrison when the presidential train arrives in the City," Winnie went on. "But I am going to do a piece on Little Jim that will cause society ladies to feel sorry for him, and they will turn to their rich husbands and demand that something be done, and their rich husbands will give money to a fund I will prepare, and Little Jim will go to the hospital and have as many operations on his leg and as many months there as are required. And that will be one botchwork thing repaired!"

She sounded quite impassioned, and she looked handsome with her back to the window and the traffic of Montgomery Street below her. I realized that I must have seen Little Jim, seated on his curbing, although no doubt he was one of the Market Street fixtures you saw but did not realize you had seen.

"I will just say to you what I have said to Tom," Bierce said, with his hands knitted together before him. "Our business as journalists, as writers, is to write well, and to write better, to write more effectively. That is our purpose, not trying to change lives, lighten burdens, and correct the mishaps of fate. That is the role of priests, preachers, and ministers, not of journalists."

"And how, may I say, would you measure your writing well and effectively, if it did not change lives and lighten burdens? Tell me that, Mr. Ambrose 'Great Cynic' Bierce?"

"Help!" Bierce said to me, grinning. "Help me with this young lady burdened with purpose!"

I said to her, "You would measure your writing skill upon the blackboard of your acquired self-knowledge, ma'am."

"Two of you!" Winnie Sweet said. Her heels rapped across the floor.

"Good luck with Little Jim," I said.

"Thank you!" she said, and was gone.

"That is a very opinionated young woman," Bierce said.

"Unlike you," I said, and seated myself to tell him what I had learned from Isabella da Costa.

"So the masked lady parading her beauties before the Stars and Stripes might be Miss da Costa, whose wish it is to become a music hall entertainer."

"It came to mind."

"And the admirable Miss Lindley knows her secrets. Can Miss Lindley be pressed?"

Not by me. Any more than Bierce could press Mrs. Hearst about the anonymous letters she had received.

"Captain Larkyn attended the revels on one occasion, but presumably never again," Bierce went on. "And another young woman, a queen-to-be like Miss da Costa, disappeared. Is there a connection?"

CHAPTER ELEVEN

RETRIBUTION, n. A rain of fire-and-brimstone that falls alike upon the just and such of the unjust as have not procured shelter by evicting them.

— *The Devil's Dictionary*

SATURDAY, MAY 22, 1891

At this time, when Bierce, in "Prattle," was not castigating the Southern Pacific Railroad, the Spring Valley Water Company, the Board of Education, politicians in general and in particular, preachers, female poets, and dogs, he was publishing fables, a form he had been working on for years. Now there was a new fable almost every week, and I had some sense of his thought processes from the direction they were taking:

> An editor who was always vaunting the purity, enterprise, and fearlessness of his paper was pained to observe that he got no subscribers. One day it occurred to him to stop saying that his paper was pure and enterprising and fearless, and make it so. "If these are good qualities," he reasoned, "it is folly to claim them."
>
> Under the new policy he got so many subscribers that his rivals endeavored to discover the secret of his prosperity, but he kept it, and when he died it died with him.

A Torch-Light Procession met a Red-Headed Girl and was extinguished in the superior effulgence.

"I think my candidate need give himself no further uneasiness in the matter," said the Red-Headed Girl passing in at the door of her house.

But the moment the door was closed the Torch-Light Procession became visible again, as brilliant as before, and the contest had to be settled with ballots, just as if God hadn't made any Girl and the Devil hadn't made any Procession.

I pondered the implications of these fables as I followed Bierce and Charles Peavine up a well-trodden trail into a canyon in the hills above Sausalito, Peavine batting at weeds with the stick he carried and Bierce pale and grim-faced from what I assumed was an asthma attack. Red-limbed manzanita branches snatched at our clothing. The trail steepened, then flattened and dipped into a dry watercourse, and steepened again. Presently we arrived in a broad space beneath the limbs of live oaks. There was a stone fire circle and boulders in a rough ring surrounding this. Bierce plumped himself down on one of these, mopping his face with his handkerchief.

"This is the place, my friends!" Peavine announced. "Here innocence was tempted by experience, and vice versa. And like all that is admirable, destroyed by its own successes." He chortled at his speech.

"It is a pretty place," I said.

"It was an exciting place with a fire blazing and the moon up over the hills, and the shadows of the branches!" Peavine seated himself on a boulder also.

"Why was Captain Larkyn not invited a second time?" Bierce asked.

"He may not have been invited the first time," Peavine said.

"I can't tell you that, for Michael Maxwell—who long ago returned to England—rather directed the festivities then."

"Taking a young woman named Flora Rodrigues with him?"

Peavine looked suddenly solemn. He shook his head. "Michael was gone before that."

"What do you think happened to her, Captain?"

"There are old mines up in the hills above us."

"Murdered, then?"

"Most people think so. She was to be queen of the Holy Ghost Festa."

"Like Miss da Costa this year," I said.

"In three weeks' time!"

A little wind off the bay caused the oak leaves to flicker in the sunlight.

"Was there any connection with the Maxwell fellow you mentioned?"

"Dunno. Don't think so."

"Captain Larkyn?"

Peavine remained silent and solemn.

"Any connection with Captain Larkyn never returning to the revels?"

"Not to speak ill of the dead," Peavine said, "Augie Larkyn was a mean, aggressive old hard-on insofar as the gentler sex was concerned. He was an embarrassment to decent folk. Gave Britishers a bad name."

"So it is possible that Larkyn made some connection with Miss Rodrigues at the revels."

"I wasn't on hand, as I say. I can only put together what I've heard."

"What about Miss Rodrigues's father? Might he be suspected of Larkyn's murder?"

"He is quite crippled, needs help getting around."

"I wonder if Billings photographed Flora Rodrigues," I said.

"His photographs of nekkid ladies?" Peavine said. "He hadn't been in Sausalito a year."

"Tell me," Bierce said. "Am I correct in assuming there was sexual activity at these affairs?"

"Some pelvic clatter, yes."

"But Captain Larkyn went beyond the bounds of propriety?"

"Filthy old sod."

"Did young ladies from New Town show up?"

"Some. You know, their life is very Old World there, and the priest is a poisonous lout out of the Middle Ages. They'd come like sightseers, some of them prepared for mild adventure also. Often they'd wear masks, but you'd know who they were."

The masked girl in Larkyn's collection, posed in front of the Stars and Stripes, had surely been Isabella da Costa. And I thought of the young women in New Town, not far below this spot, listening to the drumming and the music, and seeing the glaze of firelight and torchlight above the rim of the hill, and imagining the wild dancing of the British men and women, and even the coupling in the outer dark.

"We must look up a Mrs. Grayling," Bierce said. "Seems to have been hired by Larkyn to write the invitations for the ball."

"Good luck," Peavine said, chuckling.

"Why do you say that?"

"I doubt she'll speak to you. Close-mouthed old trot. Well, she's not old, maybe forty-odd, but she's been old all her life."

"She served as Larkyn's social secretary?"

Peavine snorted. "He didn't have any cause for a social secretary. He'd just ask her to perform some task, upon which she would curtsy and hop to it because he was out of some earldom in Suffolk, or I forget where."

"Was she a member of your revels?"

"Not a bit of it! Appalled, shocked, et cetera. She's a chum of mine, though, curiously enough."

"You specified the females of the revels as Victorian ladies casting aside their pruderies," I said. "And they are the ladies who call Tessie Powers 'dirty drawers'?"

"Is hypocrisy such a rarity in this great country?" Peavine asked, grinning at me. He said to Bierce, "What do you want of Iris Grayling?"

"A list of who was invited to the ball aboard the *Oriana,* with a check mark as to who attended. Can you get her to release such a document?"

"Aye, I'll try." He chuckled and said, "I could make a pretty good list myself, who was apt to be invited—not me, that was for certain!"

"I'd appreciate if you would do that also," Bierce said. "It would be helpful if we could compare your list with Mrs. Grayling's."

"Shall be done."

Bierce inquired again about Flora Rodrigues's parents.

"Vasco Rodrigues is a good fellow," Peavine said. "The mother is a dreary old trash heap of wrongs done her."

"We must have a talk with her," Bierce said. "Where can we find her?"

"In New Town, of course. Just ask at the pharmacy there."

———

The Rodrigueses' bungalow was the third in a block of eight of them, on a rutted dirt street, with an unkempt yard disreputable among the well-kept ones on either side. Bierce and I strode up a cracked cement walk, past a lemon tree and a spindly quince. A porch was hung with heavy moss baskets, from which no flowers bloomed. A gray-haired woman opened the door at my knock.

"We have come to speak to you of your daughter, madam," Bierce said.

"Which daughter, mister?"

"Miss Flora Rodrigues," Bierce said.

The woman stared at him. She was dark-complected, with darker flesh like stains around her eyes, but not so old as she had first appeared. Yet with an aged, shuffling motion, she backed up and swung an arm to usher us in.

The room was so dim it was moments before my eyes could make out the loom of furniture, a glint of silver on a far wall. There was a scent of dead flowers.

"Sit down, please, misters," the woman said, and remained standing while we were seated in dimly seen chairs. The glint on the wall was a silver crucifix, below it the squares of framed photographs.

"My dead daughter," Mrs. Rodrigues said.

"Do you know that she is dead?" Bierce asked.

"She is dead to me, misters."

"And why is that, madam?"

"She has told me she does not wish to be Portuguesa, she will not make her life here, she will make her life in some grand city where she will offend her parents, her people, her Savior Himself—because she was born beautiful, you see."

"I see," Bierce said.

"And I have told her she is dead to me. Her father is more forgiving than his wife, but to me she is dead."

"Tell me," Bierce said, "who was it convinced her she should make her life in some grand city?"

"She convinced herself, misters."

"That she would become famous as a singer and dancer?"

"As a whore, yes."

"All singers and dancers are whores?"

"Of the kind that she would become, misters."

She seated herself at last, the gray top of her head catching a little light from the window.

"But she was encouraged to become a singer and dancer?"

"Os Ingleses!" she said, and made a spitting sound.

"Captain Larkyn?"

"Captain Larkyn, Captain Bastable. Our Savior will not be mocked for long, misters. She danced for them aboard their sinful ships. She sang for them. I do not doubt that she whored for them."

"You are very bitter," Bierce said.

"Yes, I am bitter. But I have other children—I have my Maria who is thirteen and a pretty child but not so certain of her beauty, and a son Miguel who is a fisherman and proud to be a fisherman."

I could see that the photographs beneath the gleaming silver crucifix were of a young girl and an older young man. I was sorry for Maria, and Miguel, and their father.

"Tell me," Bierce said, leaning forward, "how was it that your daughter came to know the British yachtsmen?"

"She was very pretty, misters! And she was not modest! They searched her out, and she was very willing."

"In those days there were British and Americans who had wild parties up in the hills."

"Oh, yes; all of our young women knew of those."

"Did Flora attend them?"

"Not with my permission, you may be sure! Who knows? There was very much temptation. The drumming up the valley behind us here, the light of the fires."

"A Captain Maxwell organized them?"

"Yes. Later Captain Peavine."

"Would she have met Captain Larkyn at one of those events?"

"I do not doubt it."

"Where has she gone?" Bierce asked.

"As I say, to some grand city, to sing and dance there. Perhaps to the City of Satan!"

It was all Bierce was going to get from her. When we were taking our leave a young girl skipped up the walk to the porch, stripping a scarf from the tight coils of her hair. She wore a black-and-white schoolgirl's pinafore and blouse. She produced a sunny smile for us. Her mother put an arm around her and held her protectively tight, her bitter face split by an attempt at a smile of farewell.

"Good day, madam," Bierce said, and lifted his hat to her. So we departed.

When we had gone a way up the rutted street, he said to me, "One can only hope that young woman escaped the House of the Dead for the City of Satan."

"Yes."

He sighed and said, "Tom, we seem to be marking time waiting for the second shoe to fall."

I pointed out that two had already fallen.

"So, a third. Usually two compass points will give you direction, but the direction has been circular in this matter."

"It may be that the first shoe to fall was Flora Rodrigues."

"We await the fourth, then."

IN THE DEAD OF NIGHT

DISCOMFITURE OF A MONGOL PAWNBROKER

MISS LINDLEY OF THE STOCKTON STREET MISSION IS NOT TAKEN IN BY A SLY RUSE

Annie Laurie sees justice done San Francisco–style and the lamentable last court case of Attorney Duggan

---

Sometimes it is impossible for the indomitable Miss Lindley of the Stockton Street Mission to gain access to houses in Chinatown, for much of the property is owned by American landlords, who protect fine incomes by the same illicit and foul means as their Mongol counterparts. On this occasion they had established a small child at play with his blocks in the entryway. Miss Lindley and her friend the photographer Mr. Fenton, with their police escort, were rebuffed by the report of a "family house." But it was soon discovered that the occupants paid twenty-five cents a day to rent the child in the entryway!

In the dead of night a thirteen-year-old girl, trembling with fear, presented herself at the door of 1018 Stockton Street. Her cruel owner, a pawnbroker, had beaten her so severely that at risk of her life the terrified child had fled his premises for the rumored safety of Miss Lindley and the Stockton Street Mission.

When the pawnbroker discovered where his valuable property had taken refuge, he at once confronted the board of the Mission. Wrapped in a beautiful silken suit, he presented himself before Mrs. Chumley, President of the Board, to complain of the loss of his servant. When this failed, he demanded to present his case to the entire board at their meeting that month. Accompanied by Attorney Madigan and a group of Chinese supporters, he made an impressive entrance in his silken robes. He confronted the girl with a promise to treat her kindly if she would return to him. Her refusal was uncompromising.

The irate pawnbroker withdrew to his attorney's offices. From there came a summons for Miss Lindley and her new charge to appear in City Court. Mr. Madigan and the pawnbroker there awaited Miss Lindley, who had not brought the child.

Attorney Madigan demanded Miss Lindley's arrest for contempt of court, but Miss Lindley responded that the summons had come upon her so unexpectedly that she had had no time to prepare the child. Judge White permitted the continuance, but decreed that the girl be placed with the Chinese Consul pending the court hearing.

Miss Lindley was thus forced to drag the weeping and protesting child to the Consul General's house.

Valuable presents poured into the Consul's house for the "guest." Friends of the pawnbroker, both American and Chinese, rallied to testify to his fine character. A document bearing hundreds of signatures was presented.

Miss Lindley was given discouraging advice by Mr. Culbertson, of the Society for the Prevention of Cruelty to Children, who told her, "I fear we shall lose this case. We have only the girl's testimony against hundreds of witnesses for the pawnbroker."

But Miss Lindley did not lose hope, trusting in her Savior, whose love strengthened her. Ten days passed and again she presented herself in court. This time she had a distinguised advocate in attorney Duggan, who had insisted that all the board of the Mission and all their charges present themselves. These were able to show what care the Mission provided the rescued children.

This time the pawnbroker had chosen not to appear, and the lawyer demanded a continuance. But Mr. Duggan leaped to his feet.

"Your Honor, I demand that this child be remanded to the Christian care of the Mission, on whose part these distinguished and heartfelt testimonials have been heard. My opponent's only tactic is to call for continuance and provide testimonials in quantity rather than quality!"

He argued with such effectiveness that Judge White granted his plea, letters of guardianship were issued, and the endangered child came to spend carefree and happy days at last at the Mission.

This was sadly, however, only a few days before Attorney Duggan's helpful career was ended by a tragic, and fatal, fall down a steep staircase. His demise is deeply mourned at the Stockton Street Mission, and by those charges he had helped to free from their captivity.

ANNIE LAURIE

CHAPTER TWELVE

MALEFACTOR, n. The chief factor in the progress of the human race.
— The Devil's Dictionary

SUNDAY, MAY 23, 1891

The morning after the venture into New Town Sausalito I headed out the door of my rooming house to meet Bierce for a breakfast of oysters and eggs at the Palace Hotel and a glimpse of Little Jim. A tall fellow muffled up in a gray overcoat, with a scarf around the lower part of his face and a cap pulled down to meet it, stuck the muzzle of a revolver into my belly and muttered, "You come, mister!"

He walked close beside me as I came along with him, with an occasional prod of the revolver muzzle.

We had gone half a block when he halted, raising one hand, then both hands, turning away from me. Bierce had joined us, his revolver drawn.

"Who is this fellow, Tom?"

"Some Feng Yup, I'd guess. Wants me to come along with him."

"Who is responsible for this, my man?" Bierce asked the tall fellow.

With a loud grunt, the highbinder was off in a sprint, overcoat and scarf bellied out in the speed of his flight.

"Shall I shoot him?" Bierce inquired, but the man was already out of range, and disappeared around a corner.

"I hope this has not spoilt your appetite," he said.

"Thanks," I said, and on an intuition, "Come with me and see if there isn't more to this."

Bierce pocketed his revolver. We headed back to my rooming house together, inside and up a flight. My door was ajar six inches.

In my room a man in a black suit stood beside my typewriter table with a sheet of paper in his hand.

He was clean-shaven with yellow hair, very handsome in an almost feminine way, and he confronted us in a graceful pose, like a dancer. He was well tailored, with a fine yellow cravat and a high collar. Bierce had produced his revolver again.

The Feng Yups must be aware that I had been with Eliza in court, with her in a rescue at the City of Pekin, and conceivably with her in my rooms and bed, and that I had witnessed and written of the assassination of Sonny Bill by their gunmen, and now Frank Stone had in his hand text I had written for Annie Laurie.

It had been decided that I would not participate in a raid in Sacramento which occupied Eliza today. She would communicate directly with Winnie Sweet.

"You're Frank Stone," I said.

"And you are Thomas Redmond, who has been writing these libels for Annie Laurie in the *Examiner.*" He had the same kind of Harvard diction as Willie Hearst. Stone regarded me with glittering black eyes. He gave off a scent of hair pomade and talcum powder, as though he'd just arrived from a barbershop.

My advice to him would be to stay out of Chinatown barbershops.

"I knew your father, young Mr. Stone," Bierce said. "Let us

say I breathed some of the same air as he did, to the detriment of my lungs. So you are taking his place in the Chinatown corridors of power."

Stone rearranged his graceful slouch. He casually dropped the sheet of paper on the stack beside my typewriter. I hadn't got my wits together yet to think what it meant that he knew I was writing the Annie Laurie pieces.

He said to me, "Frankie's here to warn you that you have taken up with a prostitute in Mission clothing."

When I drew back a fist he flinched, which pleased me.

Bierce said, "This fellow was well known at Harvard for purveying the services of young females to his classmates."

"A ponce, you mean," I said.

"Indeed. I am pleased to make your acquaintance, Mr. Stone. I would like to ask you your connection with Captain Larkyn of the *Oriana*."

"I knew him, everybody knew him," Stone said with a shrug. I thought of Eliza's photograph in Larkyn's collection, and something clicked, clicked and missed.

"I wonder if you were present on the *Oriana* when he was murdered."

Stone shook his head. "Frankie can prove he was half a dozen other places than over there."

"I'm sure you can, although we will see if your name appears on the guest list. I'm interested in your mutual business with Captain Larkyn."

"I had no business with him," Stone said. Then he said to me, "Frankie's here to warn you, Redmond. Cease and desist writing these inflammatory pieces on Chinatown business. I also advise you to stay away from the prostitute in question."

"I'll bet that is the kind of letter you wrote Mrs. Hearst," I said.

Bierce blinked at me. Stone scowled handsomely.

"Ask her how she was employed in Cambridge," he said. "Ask her who she was spreading her legs for. Ask her who that big valuable fundament belongs to. Ask her, Redmond. That'll be the end of that. I'll be going!" he said to Bierce.

He started past me, taking his hat from the hook on my door and fitting it onto his yellow hair. I hit him so hard on the shoulder that he stumbled halfway across the room. Hunched against the wall beside the bureau, his eyes glittered insanely at me as he panted, then he was gone out the door.

I stretched out the fingers of the fist I had hit him with, which ached in a pleasant way, and waved my hand as though dispelling a bad smell. "Have to have the place fumigated to get the poison out." My voice sounded as though I was talking out of a barrel. But I had known, hadn't I?

"So he was the source of Mrs. Hearst's letters," Bierce said. "He has ingratiated himself with the Feng Yups. He may mean to operate the *Oliver Ferris* again. Did you know of the father?"

"I've heard of Jabez Stone."

"It was a great satisfaction when that monster lost his wits to the morbus gallicus and spent his last days howling in his agonies."

"You think this one had some connection with Captain Larkyn?"

"The father surely did. I extrapolate the son as well."

"A connection of what?"

"What I know is this: A young woman from Sausalito disappeared. Chief Casey claims there were no other such disappearances in Sausalito. I am certain that there have been such, however, in San Francisco. Some of those young women who boarded the five o'clock ferries to the festivities aboard the yachts in Sausalito did not return."

I felt a lace of sweat on my forehead. "Good God," I said.

"Yes," Bierce said. "I have set this matter before the chief of detectives here and we will see what he discovers."

"Larkyn," I said. "I think we should go to see Captain Peavine again."

"Breakfast first," Bierce said sternly.

———

Peavine's *Clio* was a couple of sizes smaller than the *Oriana*, with a red-striped weathered-looking stack. I sent a boatman out to hail Captain Peavine, and we waited for him at the Bon Ton.

Peavine sauntered in, clad in a worn blue jacket and a nautical cap so battered as to look almost a tricorn. His teeth glinted in his curly beard, but he did not look pleased.

"You have taken me away from vital maritime work, gents. I hope this is important."

"Of the utmost," Bierce said, rising to shake Peavine's hand.

Peavine gave my hand a press and jerk also. "Redmond," he said.

He seated himself with a clatter of chair legs, ordered a lager from the barkeep, and took a sheaf of papers from his jacket pocket.

These were lists: the invitation list, the longest, typewritten; a shorter one in a precise copperplate; and a third in what must have been Peavine's own hand, which was half print, half cursive. I glanced through them to see a few names I knew and many I didn't. No Frank Stone. There was Miss Eliza Lindley, and, on the invitation list, Miss Isabella da Costa. Other than that the lists did not mean much to me. Bierce pocketed them.

Bierce said, "The Portuguese young woman who disappeared, Flora Rodrigues. When we left you yesterday, as you know, we called on her mother, who insists that she is dead, although she only means her daughter has been canceled from her sympathies. It was not a rewarding encounter."

"Warned you," Peavine said.

Bierce held up a finger. "I believe also missing will be found a number of young women from San Francisco. Those who have come to Sausalito to attend celebrations aboard the yachts at the Yacht Club."

Peavine's face looked suddenly drawn. He swiped at a moustache of foam. "Ah, Jesus!" he said.

"I postulate that Larkyn was involved in this," Bierce said. "And was murdered because of that involvement."

Peavine stared at him with bright green eyes.

"What do you think, Peavine?" I said.

"That the murderer should be praised rather than pursued."

"There were two murders," Bierce said. "Will you say the other was also well deserved?"

Peavine pulled a face at me. "What's wanted, gents?" he asked.

"Why was Larkyn disinvited from the revels?"

"Already informed you that was before my time."

"I suspect you are well aware of the reasons, sir."

Peavine leaned his elbows on the table and inclined his head forward, glancing at the backs of four men seated on stools at the bar and the barkeep polishing glasses behind it. In a lowered voice he said, "What you call the revels were what they were, but there were standards and limits. Participants did not dance around with their peckers in their hands."

"Larkyn misbehaved."

"Randy old cock."

"Tell us this, then, Captain Peavine: Was Miss Flora Rodrigues a part of the revels?"

"Dunno, I told you."

"Why would she be interested in Larkyn?" I asked.

"He attracted women, no question of it. He could sell a bill of goods to a young lady who wanted out of Portygee town and knew she had the looks to make something of herself."

Like Isabella da Costa.

"You are thinking Augie did away with these young ladies?" Peavine said to Bierce in a rough voice.

Bierce, grim-lipped, did not reply.

"Do I think he was capable of it?" Peavine prodded him. "Yes, I do." He leaned back and folded his arms. "Now what?"

"Photographs," Bierce said. "It may be that Larkyn collected photographs of the young women who disappeared."

"Nekkid photographs," Peavine said, nodding.

"Mr. Hearst's photographer, Billings, was murdered the same night as Larkyn. What was the connection? You have told us it is generally known that he was taking nude photographs."

"Rumored," Peavine said.

"So then it is also rumored that one of the subjects was Miss Powers."

"No doubt."

"One more thing, Captain Peavine," Bierce said. "Do you know of any connection between Captain Larkyn and a steamship owner named Jabez Stone?"

"That rusty old tub anchored off Alcatraz right now is his. Was his." He stared at Bierce again. "Bringing in shiploads of those poor Chinese lassies, hardly more than babies. I'd like to blow that old tub out of the water. No, I don't know of any connections with Augie Larkyn, just that they were both Bluebeard toward women."

He rose suddenly. "So the son will take over the family store. You know, Jabez Stone was a stupid man, mind eaten up with the old rale. Wager the son's bright as a skylark, university fellow, and all that. Willie Hearst is used to having the fastest launch on the bay. But what about this fellow's launch I've seen a time or two? He'll be challenging the *Aquila,* no telling what all he'll be challenging, no telling what he's after! And he's acquainted with your friend Miss Lindley, I believe, Redmond?"

I did not respond and saw a flicker of his eyebrow; we had exploited his knowledge of Sausalito, the one-eyed jacks, the British colony, and the Portuguese, and it seemed to me that he was showing that he knew about us, too— me, anyway, Eliza anyway—and that I had better understand that he must not be underestimated.

"Back to my chores, gents," he said, and with a farewell flip of his hand seemed unable to get out of the Bon Ton Saloon fast enough.

———

Bierce was unable to persuade Chief Casey to let us take the photographs of the females from Larkyn's collection back to the San Francisco detective bureau, but promised that he would deliver them there himself.

CHAPTER THIRTEEN

ULTIMATUM, n. In diplomacy, a last demand before resorting to concessions.

> — *The Devil's Dictionary*

MONDAY, MAY 24, 1891

TREACHERY IN SACRAMENTO

ATTEMPT TO BUSHWHACK THE DIRECTRIX OF THE STOCKTON STREET MISSION IN THE STATE CAPITAL

HOW MISS LINDLEY WAS NEARLY TRICKED BY A VICIOUS PLOT OF MONGOL SLAVERS AND SACRAMENTO POLICE

An adventure in the State Capital in which Miss Lindley displays ingenuity and fortitude to thwart her enemies

Miss Lindley of the Stockton Street Mission followed the trail of a kidnapped Chinese girl child to Sacramento, where she had been warned not to let her whereabouts be known even to the police of the State Capital. She recalled the early days of her Mission when she had not known whom she could trust—not even policemen, not even judges, certainly not attorneys, and above all not the loquacious and seemingly high-minded Chinese who assured her that these poor enslaved souls were happy, well treated, and also relatives, even daughters, saved from starvation and worse in old China.

The note she had received informed her that she was to call at a certain address in Chinatown near the river. Until the appointed moment Miss Lindley was sequestered in a room in the fine old Garrett Hotel across from the Capitol. She hired a carriage to take her to the heart of Chinatown in the cool of evening. While the hack waited she hastened inside the narrow two-story menacing old building. There was her quarry, a beautiful black-haired child, holding a bundle wrapped in a silk scarf. Miss Lindley clutched her hand and they fled to the hack, and, calling for the utmost speed of which the animals were capable, back to the hotel. But how to get her new charge to San Francisco, as there was no train that night?

The night clerk knocked on her door to warn her that a policeman had come to him inquiring about a white woman and a Chinese girl. He urged Miss Lindley to leave town, for corrupt police officers were in the pay of the tong rulers. He offered to row her across the river himself. But she could not trust him. She trusted, as she had always had to trust, her "intuition." She knew there was a milk train at dawn. She and the child spent the night in her room, quaking at any sound of footsteps in the carpeted hallway. At the first gray light she roused her sleeping ward. Together they crept down the back stairs and dashed through deserted streets in the morning mists off the river just in time to astonish the conductor, who had rarely seen travelers on this early route, and never before a young white woman with a shivering Chinese girl in tow.

And so they reached San Francisco in safety, but Miss Lindley realized the danger that had threatened her, and vowed never again to mount her expeditions of rescue without the protection the City's police and detective bureaus were so ready to provide.

ANNIE LAURIE

I was with Eliza at the Mission when her friend Matthew Fenton called. He was a white-haired little man of about fifty, with a hairless, opossum kind of face fitted with a jut of white whiskers like an afterthought. His territory as a photographer was Chinatown, Chinese faces, Chinese scenes. Eliza had told me he had an opium addiction.

After shaking my hand, he said, "Liza, did Annie Laurie accompany you to Sacramento?"

Eliza sat at her desk, eyeglasses on; behind her head was the sign: I CAN DO ALL THINGS THROUGH CHRIST WHICH STRENGHTHENETH ME.

She shook her head. "I told her what had transpired there. I think Tom will agree with me, that the news in the *Examiner* is not always fact."

"That is an unhappy fact," I said.

Fenton paced up and down before her desk, head down. "Liza, you are in danger. I have been warned of it by half a dozen people."

He gave me an unfriendly glance. He did not like me much, though I didn't think it was because of an attachment to Eliza. She said he was just a good friend who liked to give her advice.

"You must be careful," he went on. "I think you must desist

on these adventures for a time. You will find your enemies are preparing for you."

"This is the last piece Miss Sweet will write this month," Eliza said.

"Your alliance with her has not been healthy," Fenton said. "Many people read the *Examiner,* and they are not all of them your friends. Tom, I am aware that this must have been arranged by your contrivance, but I am afraid the wide publication of these efforts of Liza's have put her in a bad position."

"On the contrary," Eliza said. "Miss Sweet's efforts have brought in many contributions to the Mission."

"I am afraid that the board and Mrs. Chumley will find that money was more hard-earned than they would wish," Fenton said.

"What do you mean?"

"You know Duggan fell downstairs to his death. Are we sure he was not assisted? Tom, I charge you with her protection!"

He stamped on out. Eliza gazed after him expressionlessly.

"How did Duggan die?" I asked.

"He was intoxicated and fell down the stairs at his hotel."

"Maybe Fenton's right," I said.

"Will you come with me?" she asked, rising.

"Where?"

"There is a child—"

"I'm not going. You're not going."

She stood frowning at me. "I will have to get Perkin, then."

"Sit down."

She seated herself, straight-backed, tight-lipped.

"There was an attempt to betray you in Sacramento. You heard Fenton just now. Yesterday I was accosted by a Chinese gunman who was going to take me somewhere, but Bierce intervened. We returned to find Frank Stone in my rooms, examining pages I had written that reveal the fact that I have been working with Miss Sweet."

"Of course he told you about me."

I nodded.

"Won't you sit down, Tom?"

I sat down facing her. I hated myself. The tip of her tongue appeared, to moisten her lower lip.

"I told you that I'd been in love with him," she said. "He had a business at Harvard. He furnished women to his classmates. I was one of them."

"That is what he said."

"I was twenty. My husband had died. I was penniless with a two-year-old child."

I said, "You told me you'd had a life before this one. I'd thought you would tell me about yourself in your own time." I looked down and said, "I can't say it's none of my business."

"And why would that be? " Eliza said.

"My affections are involved."

"Mine are also involved, you know."

"He was your paramour?"

"Yes, Tom. Before my employment, and during it. I'm sorry if you are distressed. I put off telling you. I'm sorry you find me to be a whited sepulchre."

"You are the beloved directress of the Stockton Street Mission, and my beloved."

She took a handkerchief from a drawer and daubed at her eyes. "It was not hard usage as far as the college boys were concerned. They were sweet, shy boys. He is a very ruthless man, however."

"Maybe I'll kill him," I said.

"Please don't speak like that on these premises!"

I regarded her pale, proud, humiliated face with her pink lips and fine nose and blurred blue eyes, and the sweep of her hair across her brow.

"Were there photographs?" I asked.

"Yes, there were," she said. "I'm sorry," she said again.

I thought it would be very easy to say the wrong thing, so I waved my hands as though dispelling a waft of overheated air.

"What can we say now?" Eliza said.

"We can say that both you and I are presently in danger from the Feng Yups and Frank Stone, and you will take no chances for the time being."

"And it is you who will decide that duration?"

"Yes," I said.

"Have you considered that you may be in more danger than I? Because they now know you have had a hand in the Annie Laurie articles, and have yourself published pieces with the same injustices in mind. And because they know you have an intimacy with me, which we were foolish to hope no one was aware of."

Upstairs there began a rhythmic chanting, the girls pronouncing English words in concert. The taut corners of Eliza's lips relaxed a little.

"I am not so fearful for myself as I am for you. He wants you to come back to him, and I am afraid that—" I stopped there.

"Never!" A pink flush swept up her cheeks. With a flick of her tongue over her lower lip again, she said, "I think it is a deep insult to him that someone should have belonged to him body and soul and then broke free. It is an abiding rebuke that my Savior should have enabled me to free myself. And then that I should come to prefer another to his charms. Tom, if I pray sometimes in the night it is not because I am tempted."

"I am sorry to trouble you with these questions. Some things I have understood, others I have not."

"Let us speak of everything, then. Now that we have opened these shameful gates."

"Were there other young women in a similar position with him?"

"Three, sometimes four."

"In a similar—thrall?"

"He assured me not. I think he assured them of the same things of which he assured me."

Upstairs the girls chanted in their shrill voices.

"Tell me," I said, "was Tessie Powers one of them?"

She did not answer right away, glancing up to meet my eyes. "I don't know," she said. "I know that he knew her. She was a barmaid at Swithin's when I knew her. Later she took up with William Hearst."

"Captain Larkyn had a photograph of her in his collection."

"Did he?" After a pause, she said, "Did he have one of me, Tom?"

"Yes."

"Frank made photographs, as I said. Nothing very indiscreet."

I covered my face with my hands. There were other questions I must ask, but something in me had rebelled.

"Eliza, come with me to my place for a little while."

"I'll just tell Miss Cochran I'm going out," she said rising quickly.

———

In the morning when I opened my door I almost stepped on a rat lying just outside in the hall, a gray corpse with its hairless tail and a patch of dried blood on its muzzle. I stepped over it, and knocked on the basement door to tell Mr. Barker to get rid of the thing.

CHAPTER FOURTEEN

LIFE, n. A spiritual pickle preserving the body from decay. We live in daily apprehension of its loss; yet when lost it is not missed. The question, "Is Life worth living?" has been much discussed; particularly by those who think it is not, many of whom have written at great length to support their view and by careful observance of the laws of health, enjoyed for long terms of years the honors of successful controversy.
— *The Devil's Dictionary*

TUESDAY, MAY 25, 1891

From the steps of the Hearst mansion, the bay spread out from the headlands of Marin to the eastern shores. Bierce and I were ushered inside by a maid with a profile out of Egypt. We passed through high, dim rooms into a chintz-and-lace parlor, where a not-young lady in a much ruffled and ribboned dress put down the newspaper she had been reading and folded her pince-nez, rising to greet us. Mrs. Hearst was short and a little stout, with the face of a fading china doll and a determined wedge of chin.

"Ah, Mr. Bierce," she said. "How kind of you to call."

I was introduced. We were asked to sit, and coffee was ordered.

"Mrs. Hearst," Bierce said, "I have it from a source that will have to be nameless that there has been an attempt to black-mail you."

Mrs. Hearst gazed at him with her lips drooping open. Her eyes clouded with anger, then with interest.

"Why, Mr. Bierce, what a detective you are!"

"Reason tells me you have been sent a photograph that would be a source of embarrassment to your son and to his female friend."

"I can't imagine how you came to know of this," Mrs. Hearst said, and rose again and bustled out of the room with a whisper of skirts. The maid brought coffee, sugar, and cream on a tray, to which Bierce and I helped ourselves.

On a gleaming grand piano was a photograph of Willie Hearst in a collegiate striped jacket and cap. Behind it filmy drapes moved in a breeze from a window opening. A brownish painting on the wall facing us displayed two deer drinking at a forest pond, while a noble white-throated stag stood guard behind them.

Mrs. Hearst returned with the photograph, which Bierce examined before passing it to me. It was as my father had described it, naked Tessie Powers as though offering a box to a front-viewed naked James Dix. The Tessie Powers likeness was the same that we had seen in Larkyn's collection.

I looked closely for a line between the two figures, and could make it out as a slight variation in the shading of the background.

"They've been stuck together," I said to Bierce.

"How can that be done, Tom?"

"Two photographs fitted together and then rephotographed to look like one image." I pointed out the indistinct line where the shade of the backstop changed.

"That had occurred to me," Mrs. Hearst said, who had reseated herself.

"The man is James Dix, Billings's model," I said. "Both Miss Powers and James Dix posed for Billings's series of nude figures engaged in mundane tasks."

"That is true, madam," Bierce said.

"I have no doubt of that, Mr. Bierce, but I believe Miss Powers should have been more concerned that these photographs would fall into the wrong hands."

"What have the wrong hands demanded?" Bierce asked.

"The photograph was delivered by a messenger. No demand has come."

"It may be something else beside a demand for money."

Mrs. Hearst looked worried.

"Have you shown this to your son?"

"I have not."

"As far as we can make out, the photographic plates were stolen from Billings's laboratory and darkroom. By his murderer, or someone else. Captain Larkyn was murdered the same night. There may have been a connection between Captain Larkyn's libidinous proclivities and the nude photographic series that engaged Billings. Or not. There were also in years past somewhat Dionysian revels that took place in the hills behind Sausalito. Nudity may have been a part of the proceedings, and perhaps photography as well."

"Good heavens!" Mrs. Hearst said, clasping her hands together before her bosom. "To think that I was relieved that Willie had chosen to make his residence in a more bucolic setting than the City!"

"There is more, madam," Bierce said calmly. "There is the disappearance of a young woman who was to be queen of the Portuguese festival of the Holy Ghost five years ago, and what seems to have been the grave danger of the present young woman chosen queen."

"You have surely been at work, Mr. Bierce!" Mrs. Hearst

produced a wintry smile. "How are these young women involved?"

"I believe Captain Larkyn was a considerable villain. But there may be others who were party to his misdeeds."

"Captain Larkyn was murdered by an avenger, you think?"

"A righteous man perhaps."

"And poor Mr. Billings?"

"Surely by the same hand," Bierce said.

"I will tell you something," Mrs. Hearst said. "When William first became involved with this young woman, at Harvard, I began receiving anonymous letters. There were five of them. I have destroyed them. I suspect they were by the same hand that sent me this photograph."

"It would be very helpful to us to know what was in those letters," Bierce said.

"They were quite vile," Mrs. Hearst said. "Need I say more?"

"Vile as to the character of Miss Powers?"

"Yes. And as to my son's relation with her."

"What was the motive, I wonder?" Bierce mused.

"I wonder also," Mrs. Hearst said.

"Did you ever meet a young man named Frank Stone at Harvard?" I asked.

She frowned, and thought, and said she thought not.

————

We had been invited to a musicale at Sea Point that evening, and we crossed the bay from the Jackson Street wharf in the *Aquila*. Willie stood at the wheel, tall and narrow-backed with his yachting cap slanted across his forehead, observed by pretty Tessie Powers, who was seated gracefully beside him on a leather cushion. She was surrounded by packets and bags, for she had spent the day shopping in the City. Bierce and I were seated on the cushions opposite her.

Now we were passing Alcatraz on this gray afternoon, with

the fog already lifted over the western coastline. Willie steered as though the horizontal blaze of sun through the Golden Gate was the ultimate destination. The *Oliver Ferris* came in sight, ladder over the side, a dinghy secured there. I saw Miss Powers glance at it without interest, Willie gazing straight ahead through the matched windows.

"Oh, look, Willie!" Miss Powers said in her sweet voice.

Another launch had appeared on the starboard quarter, bone in her teeth, not so big a boat as the *Aquila,* with a red superstructure, a black hull, a fat yellow stack spouting smoke.

"Oh, my gracious!" Willie said, and, hunching a little in his intensity, reached a long pale hand for the accelerating lever.

The racket of the steam engine increased. The acceleration pushed me back in my seat. "We'll see about this!" Willie exclaimed.

But the other launch came on. It must have been already at peak revolutions, while the *Aquila* was still in the acceleration process. The launch came closer on the starboard side, an indistinct figure visible through the windows of the cabin. I saw Miss Powers tense, stare, and suddenly drop her eyes to her lap.

The two launches churned on across the gray bay, the new one inching a little farther forward, then no farther, then almost imperceptibly falling back. Willie Hearst glanced back at it with his teeth clenched.

It was impossible to speak over the churn of the engine. I touched Bierce's knee, flicked a finger to indicate Miss Powers, then at the figure in the launch, and leaned back. Bierce cast a look toward the other launch as the *Aquila* pulled triumphantly away.

"I thought I knew all the launches on the bay!" Willie shouted over the racket of the steam engine. "On the coast," he added.

Tessie Powers stared straight ahead with a set chin.

"Tessie, that surely looked like Chink Stone," Willie said in a grating voice.

"You know I am nearsighted, Willie," she said.

———

After a stroll around town, and a glass or two at the Bon Ton while night fell, Bierce and I mounted the steps toward the high lighted windows of Sea Point, where faint piano notes grew louder. Ah Sook, in his white tunic, bowed us inside and we were installed on the veranda and offered refreshments, while the piano playing continued. When there was a pause, we were ushered into a large main room, whence the music had come. A dark-haired woman sat at the piano; a gent in a dinner jacket held a fiddle. Willie Hearst beckoned us to chairs among six or eight others, none of whom I recognized, but some of whom must have been the good folks Brits of Casey's judgment. The pianist played with a good deal of arm motion, the fiddler stroked his bow, and the music was pleasant enough. When it ceased, the fiddler bowed and the assembled clapped.

"Tessie will dance," Willie Hearst whispered to Bierce, behind his hand. He was dressed in soup and fish, with a white bow tie stiff as a lath beneath his chin.

And when the fiddler sounded another note, and the dark-haired pianist bent to her keyboard, Tessie Powers slipped in through a side door. She was clad in veils that fluttered and settled around her person like colored breezes, delineating her body rather than exposing it. Her hair was done up in a kind of crown decorated with flowers, two curved cheek pieces framing her solemn face as she placed a foot and swayed, curvetted, and high-stepped with her hands on her waist and gazing searchingly right and left. I thought she was beautiful, and that she was well aware of it.

Bierce sat with his fingers tented together. Willie watched his inamorata with an expression of pride on his pale, long-nosed face. The musicians played and Tessie danced, her face bright with the exertion. When she had finished, curtsying deeply, Willie led the applause.

————

When the other guests had departed, Bierce and I remained with Willie in a sitting room with windows gazing out on the black of the bay dotted with lights.

"Miss Powers is very accomplished," Bierce said.

"She loves to dance," Willie Hearst said. "It is unfortunate that we live at a time when expressive dancers are looked upon with disfavor."

"Tell me," Bierce said, "did Miss Powers once dance for a gathering of the local subjects of Queen Victoria?"

"Yes, she did," Willie said shortly. "It was a great error on my part. Not that one wishes to be a member of their nasty-minded little British Benevolent Society, but that damned evening seems to have made Tessie a despicable object in their sour estimations. I very much regret it. She is insufferably cut on every visit to the shops.

"Of course, they are prejudiced against anything unfamiliar, such as an irregular marital situation," Willie added, as though he had guessed my thoughts.

"A prejudice your mother shares," Bierce said.

"Yes, she does," Willie said.

"Are these locals aware that Miss Powers was posing nude for your photographer?"

"It is possible," Willie said.

"Someone was aware of it, who broke in to steal the photographic plates."

Willie sighed. "That is obvious, Mr. Bierce."

"As far as we could make out, Larkyn possessed only one print. Tell me, could his interest in Miss Powers have had to do with her desire to dance?"

"He was present on that regrettable evening."

"Nothing more?"

"You must ask her," Willie said, rising as Miss Powers came into the sitting room, attired now in a long black skirt and a white high-necked, long-sleeved blouse. She still wore her hair in the crownet decorated with silk rosebuds. The cheek pieces framed her pretty face. Bierce and I also rose.

"You have won two more enthusiasts with your artistry, my dear," Willie said. He had a quality of sometimes seeming no more than a boy, and sometimes a very sophisticated gentleman, as now. Perhaps it was his position as master of a mistress. It was a position, I realized, that I now shared.

"Thank you, Willie. Gentlemen." Miss Powers seated herself in the wicker chair beside Willie's.

"That was very graceful and accomplished, Miss Powers," Bierce said, and I echoed him.

"Mrs. Potts played the piano so well, and Mr. Bell was at his best tonight!"

"Mr. Bierce has a question for you, my dear."

She leaned forward so as to gaze at Bierce past Willie.

"Perhaps more than one," Bierce said. "To begin with, did Captain Larkyn's interest in you have to do with an interest in dancing on his part?"

She colored. "Yes, it did, Mr. Bierce. He claimed that a cousin was the owner of a very famous music hall in London, and that he himself was well acquainted with impresarios in the City."

"And proposed to introduce you to these acquaintances?"

"Yes, he did; exactly. But, Mr. Bierce, it is a proposition well understood by young women who are no longer naive."

Willie laughed delightedly.

"Miss Powers, I understand that you met Mr. Hearst in Cambridge. Tell me, were you acquainted with a man named Frank Stone there?"

Miss Powers's features changed from pink to pale and she sank back in her chair until her face was hidden.

"Yes, I knew Frank Stone," she whispered.

"Frank Stone was a classmate of mine," Willie said in a flat voice. "His father was Jabez Stone, the shipping fellow. Frank had to leave Harvard when his father became sick. I believe there was some loss of fortune."

Bierce glanced sideways at me, which I took as permission, so I said to Willie Hearst, "Did you know that Frank Stone had a lucrative sideline that was the cause of his dismissal from Harvard?"

"He left Harvard because of family financial problems," Willie said stubbornly.

Tessie sat back in her chair, her fingers knitted together before her breast.

"I do not believe this line of investigation will take us anywhere," Willie said to Bierce, in his adult-decisive voice.

And Bierce inclined his head in agreement, but not, I thought, in capitulation.

CHAPTER FIFTEEN

SCRIPTURES, n. The sacred books of our holy religion, as distinguished from the false and profane writings on which all other faiths are
based.

— The Devil's Dictionary

WEDNESDAY, MAY 26, 1891

In the warm dark, in my bed in my rooms on Sacramento
Street, I said to my invisible companion, "My mother demands
grandchildren."

"It is a responsibility," Eliza said in my ear.

Indeed I had a son, who would be four now, whom I could
never publicly call my own or gratify my mother with. I had
performed a service for a friend whose husband could not give
her a child because of an old illness.

"I have sworn I will never break her heart," I said.

"How would that be accomplished, my dear?"

"By marrying outside the Church."

She giggled, a sound so foreign to her that I was shocked.

"Well, then, you must marry a papist female and get her
with child. Does that seem so difficult to you?"

"It does right now," I said.

"Show me how you would go about it," Eliza whispered.

———

Later she said, "I was raised by papists."

It was what Father Flanagan had guessed. "Your mother and father?"

"Father and stepmother."

"And now you are a Protestant?"

"The Mission saved my soul. That would be one's religion, wouldn't it, where one has found salvation?"

"And here you are," I said.

"Yes," she said, and did not sound pleased that I had said that. And I was ashamed that I had said it.

"Maybe you are my salvation," I said.

THURSDAY, MAY 27, 1891

The next morning Bierce and I sat at the scarred oak table in the corner of the Bon Ton Saloon waiting for Charles Peavine.

I did not wish to bring Eliza Lindley into Bierce's speculations, so I kept my own counsel as to the fact that Miss Lindley of the Stockton Street Mission had been one of the girls Frank Stone hired out at Cambridge. It must be that Tessie Powers had been one of them also, and Willie Hearst knew it.

Peavine came in wearing canvas pants, a blue work shirt, and a bandana knotted around his neck. His teeth gleamed in his red-gold beard as he shook hands. He seated himself and signaled for a lager.

"What can I do for you, gents?"

"How can we board the *Oliver Ferris*?" Bierce asked, leaning forward.

"And why would you want to do that, Mr. Bierce?"

"Looking for evidence of the villainy of Captain Larkyn."

Peavine swigged his beer. "Tell you what," he said. "I can't take the *Clio* out there for your boarding party; she'd stand out like a bridesmaid on a pile of manure. But let me see if Rudy Carvalho will help." He rose and was gone.

"The vanished young women," Bierce said, "would not be females of circumstances that would create much outcry. The Detective Bureau has declined to be of assistance. I am in bad odor there. I've asked Mammy Pleasant to see what she can find out about them and their aspirations."

Mammy Pleasant was Bierce's informational ally, the ultimate source on San Francisco high life and low life.

"For instance, were they interested in dancing?" I said.

"Did they hope to become music hall entertainers?" Bierce added.

"Larkyn's murderer should be given a medal."

"Perhaps."

"What of a connection between Larkyn and Frank Stone?"

"I believe that the exploitation of women is a pitch that defiles, a liquor that endrunkens, a poison that penetrates the bones," Bierce said, in a burst of pomposity.

"Exploitation?" I said.

"A commerce in exploitation."

Peavine returned, and seated himself with a kind of flourish of handling the chair and arranging his limbs to conform to it. "Rudy Carvalho owes me a favor," he said.

"Why is that?" I asked.

"A dead whale washed up on the beach over at New Town, where the Portygees live—stunk to high heaven. As president of the festival, it's Rudy's duty to protect the welfare of the faithful during his watch, so he requested that the *Clio* tow the beast out to the Farallons to dump it.

"Hold on," he said suddenly. "Someone you should meet."

A Portuguese fellow swung into the Bon Ton on two crutches, sunburnt face beneath grizzled hair. He was headed for the bar when Peavine intercepted him, spoke to him at some length unheard by us, and headed him our way.

Peavine introduced him as Vasco Rodrigues, and the man propped one crutch under his arm and shook hands with a grip that would have crushed Willie Hearst's limp lily of a handshake. He greeted us with an expression of great sweetness.

"'Allo, gentemen," he said in heavily accented English.

Peavine helped settle him at the table. A beer was ordered for him.

"You have see my wife, Sharlee say-ez."

"We have," Bierce said. "We wished to ask about your daughter. She told us the girl is dead to her."

Rodrigues said with his sweet smile, "Alive to me!"

Bierce looked surprised. "You know where she is, sir?"

"I do!"

"Where may I find her?"

"Ah!" Finger to his lips, he said, "I have swear I will not tell. But is alive to me, and she do ver' well!"

The theory of August Larkyn as a murderer of young women had taken a punch in the solar plexus.

"She is an entertainer?" Bierce asked.

Rodrigues glanced puzzled at Peavine, then back to Bierce, "She sing!"

"In the City?" I asked.

Peavine said, "I promised that you would not grill him on this matter, Redmond."

"She is one fine young lady, gentemen," Rodrigues said, smiling. "Her father ver' proud. My wife, she do not know, she do not want to know." His face discomposed with sorrow. His crutch scraped against the side of his chair, and Peavine reached out to steady it.

"Vasco accepts the young woman's profession, his wife does not," Peavine said.

"Clearly," I said. I wished to feel relieved rather than disappointed.

"Mus' go," Rodrigues said, struggling to his feet. "Farewell, gentemen." Peavine helped him arrange his crutches. He swung back to the bar with some celerity.

Presently Captain Carvalho arrived, such a neat, erect, self-contained little fellow that he made me feel large and clumsy. He was about fifty, wearing a black double-breasted nautical suit with gold buttons, a striped necktie, and a captain's cap carried underarm. He had a handlebar moustache streaked with gray, and jet-black hair. He nodded to Bierce and me, and clicked his heels. We shook hands.

Charles Peavine explained our wish.

Carvalho seated himself, frowning, and said, "This would be a day for such an action, sirs. Thursdays the watch leaves the ship unattended and proceeds into the City for supplies, and in the usual case will spend some time in saloons there."

"Ought to be prosecuted," Peavine said sternly. "So you have been observing, Rudy?"

"One observes," Carvalho said in his unaccented English. "One observes and comes to summations. It is a ship of evil."

"What evil would that be, Captain Carvalho?"

"There are many rumors, sir."

"Besides bringing in slave girls from Canton Province?" I asked.

Instead of responding, he said, "Tell me, sirs: why would this evil ship be anchored out in the bay where it can be observed by all?"

"I will answer you thus, Captain Carvalho," Bierce said. "It is anchored in plain sight so as to show that it is not presently involved in the evils you mention but do not delineate."

Captain Carvalho nodded, as at the correct answer. "Charles does not wish to steam out in the beautiful *Clio*?" he asked.

"Too observable," Peavine said.

"I will provide less luxurious transportation," Carvalho said. "Charles, you will show the gentlemen where to meet me?"

"I will, Rudy," Peavine said.

————

Carvalho's *Ysabel* was a fishing craft about thirty feet long, everything aboard neat and stowed in a redolence of fish and tar, a lateen sail, and his mop-headed son at the tiller. Carvalho, Bierce, Peavine, and I took seats along the rails. With the sail snapping above us we passed the pale cliffs of Alcatraz and slanted toward the *Oliver Ferris,* riding her anchor prow-on against the eastern shore.

The mop-headed son, a cigarillo slanting from his jaw, swung the *Ysabel* perfectly against the rusty flank of the old hulk, where a rope ladder trailed its ends into the gray bay. Carvalho shipped the sail and Peavine rose with the line Carvalho handed him to secure the boat. We mounted the ladder with Peavine holding the floppy rope contraption steady.

On deck Carvalho exclaimed with disgust, for all was foul and clutter, with sprung coils of rope, twists of cable, bundles of stained canvas, and chunks of rusted machinery set out on the greasy decking.

A track of woven hemp led aft toward the iron-walled superstructure with a clerestory of panes of filthy glass above it.

An iron door was strapped open above a high threshold with a bit of rope. The space inside must have been the captain's cabin, for it had once been outfitted with surprising luxury, the high windows letting in the afternoon light, a large bed with tangled blankets and pillows that had been used recently, a torn and sagging bedstead canopy, the personal effects of the watchman scattered on a deal table and a dresser, a sumptuous armoire with a broken door against one wall, a dim brown painting with a golden frame beside it—an altogether curious room. The place stunk of what must have been a full commode under the bed. Bierce and I stamped around within the cabin. Bierce peered distastefully into the closet, and I opened the drawers of the dresser, which contained only a seaman's garb and gear.

In a right-hand drawer I found a curious object, a kind of mask made of reddish leather, more a head covering than a mask, a rooster head, with a cock's comb, and a yellow beak made of a stiffer leather. It was a horrid object, greasy to the touch, and I showed it to Bierce, then jammed it back into its drawer.

Carvalho and Peavine had not come inside with us, but had disappeared down a companionway.

When we left the cabin Bierce bent to examine the lock of the roped-open door. "Look here!"

Where the inner latch should have been was a smooth patch of steel about a foot long, no handle. The latch was on the outside, nothing on the inside.

Bierce freed the door. He closed it, rattled the handle and opened it again, roping it back. I stared at the patch of steel, appalled at its implications.

"Where have our nautical friends disappeared to?" Bierce said.

We followed along the passageway in increasing darkness, a smoky illumination ahead. Peavine had found a bull's-eye lantern and flashed its light around another room, small and windowless, with an iron sink in one corner on rusted legs, and a long table adjoining it, on which were some metal canisters.

"What the devil do you suppose this place was?" Peavine wanted to know. "I've never seen a room like this aboard ship. There was some special function—"

"It is a darkroom for producing photographic images," Bierce said.

"What is that you are thinking, sir?" Carvalho said.

"I think photographs were taken in the main cabin, and developed here."

No one asked what kind of photographs.

On deck again Bierce looked exhausted, cheeks lined, hat pulled down on his head. He leaned on the rail gazing toward Alcatraz Island. Carvalho sat on a stanchion, grim-faced beneath his natty cap, pulling at one horn of his moustache. Below us the *Ysabel* rocked against the flank of the *Oliver Ferris,* the son smoking in the stern. A square-rigger passed under tow on the south side of Alcatraz, the tug emitting a high trail of smoke.

Peavine and I with the bull's-eye lantern searched through the rest of that rusty hulk, and found nothing of interest. I was conscious of the heaviness of my heart because it lightened as the *Ysabel* pulled away and tacked toward Sausalito. I noticed that no one looked back.

"Billings was killed in error," Bierce announced.

"Making nekkid photographs there at Sea Point," Peavine said, leaning against the rail with his legs crossed and his arms folded on his chest. "Everybody in town knew it."

"If everybody in town knows a thing it is most usually untrue," Bierce said. "Billings was doing just what Willie assumed he was doing, taking photographs of bodies in motion—James's and Miss Powers's."

"If you will pardon me, Mr. Bierce," Carvalho said. "These liknesses have had some circulation. They are sold and traded in Sausalito and San Francisco. Our young men have come into possession of them. Formerly they were everywhere to be seen."

"What likenesses?" Bierce inquired.

"Likenesses of unclothed young women, sir!"

"But not recently, you say?" Bierce inquired.

Carvalho considered, frowned, and nodded.

"Billings had not been here a year," Bierce said.

There was silence as we sailed on toward Sausalito.

"That cabin and that darkroom are places one could wish he'd never seen, friends," Peavine said.

I agreed with him.

CHAPTER SIXTEEN

REPROBATION, n. In theology, the state of a luckless mortal prenatally damned. The doctrine of reprobation was taught by Calvin, whose joy in it was somewhat marred by the sad sincerity of his conviction that although some are foredoomed to perdition, others are predestined to salvation.

— The Devil's Dictionary

FRIDAY, MAY 28, 1891

Mammy Pleasant had become Ambrose Bierce's ally because she perceived that he was sympathetic to the cause of her race, to which cause she herself was passionately attached. In earlier years in San Francisco, blacks were prohibited from attending public schools, and from riding on the street and cable cars. She was arrested several times for violating this ordinance, but was never prosecuted. This may have been because she was widely feared as a practitioner of voodoo magic and had been a student of the notorious Marie LaVeau of New Orleans, and because in her practice of helping people of her race find employment in the mansions on Nob Hill, South Park, and the peninsula, she was the recipient of many secrets. In her youth she had passed for white and was reputed to have been beautiful. She was a supporter of John Brown, and had come to the

West Coast when the South became dangerous for her. She was in her time a famous cook and served in that capacity in some of San Francisco's aristocratic establishments. As housekeeper for one of the City's financial wizards, she had built a small fortune for herself, which had been wiped out in the failure of the Bank of California. She had owned laundries and boarding-houses, houses of assignation and plain parlor houses, and had been rumored to be a "baby-farmer," supplying babies when they were needed and disposing of them when they were not.

That was all years ago. These days she was only an old and rather sinister presence to be encountered downtown in the City, hunched and hurrying in her cloak and bonnet that contained a grim dark face, and carrying her large covered baby-sized basket.

Now she sat in Bierce's office, poking a bony finger at an eye-hole of the skull on his desk. Although she rarely smiled, her face was, at least for her, amiable. She had removed her bonnet to reveal a head covered with graying curls. Bierce leaned back in his desk chair, and I sat on the other side. Down the hall was the cheerful bellowing and response that was one of the pleasures of a position at Willie Hearst's Monarch of the Dailies.

"You have asked me for information on these young women that have disappeared," she said. "It has been four, five years ago now and I have not learned much. Two of them was an Esther Rogers and a Madeleine Kelly."

"They were young women who came to Sausalito for the Saturday night entertainments aboard the yachts there?"

"Would have been, yes. Others also, but I have some track of these."

"And these hoped for theatrical careers?"

"The Rogers woman in particular. The other was a singer in the choir at St. Bartholomew's."

"Is it thought that they were murdered?"

"Never seen hide nor hair of them again." Mammy Pleasant thrust out her sharp chin like a weapon.

"Tell me this, Mrs. Pleasant. Have you ever heard of a ship in the bay where indecent photographs were made?"

"Property of old Jabez Stone when he was alive," she said, nodding. "I disremember the name of it."

"The *Oliver Ferris*?"

"Maybe so."

"What do you know about it?"

"Fancy gents went there for other business. There was a bunch of photographs of girls and men sold around town. Don't know who the women were."

"Esther Rogers and Madeleine Kelly, among others?"

Mammy Pleasant shrugged and hunched forward over her side of the desk, patting the skull on its dome.

"Old Jabez Stone's son been rummaging around to get that old ship renovated," she said. "Be headed for the Candlestick Point Shipyard sometime soon. Appears he has come onto some money."

"From the Feng Yups?"

"I heard it that his daddy had buried some money up in the Oakland Hills, and the young man figured out where it was. He has bought himself a steam launch and can put on some dog. They say he is a wizard among young women."

I tried not to think about that.

Mammy Pleasant donned her bonnet, hefted her big basket as though it contained considerable weight, and departed.

"She is invaluable," Bierce said to me. "Especially since I seem to be in chancery with the Detective Bureau."

"So we know there were white women captive aboard the *Oliver Ferris,* as well as Chinese children."

"Jabez Stone was the proprietor, August Larkyn the recruiter."

"And now Junior has resumed his father's associations. For the same purposes?"

Bierce took a deep breath. "We are a nation of vulgarians floundering in a sea of public and private corruption. But rarely does one perceive so efficient and purposeful an *evil*."

Frank Stone had been Eliza Lindley's pimp in Cambridge, and it was clear he had had an association with Tessie Powers as well, because of which he had written the anonymous letters to Mrs. Hearst. I did not mention my thoughts to Bierce because they were too close to the bone.

"What are we going to do?" I said.

"Our purpose is to recover the missing photographic plates. which may or may not have to do with the murdered August Larkyn, but surely have to do with the murder of Billings. I propose that we hew to that purpose."

———

I escorted Eliza to dinner at a ristorante on Montgomery Street, where platters of steaming pasta borne past us increased our appetites and brought color to Eliza's cheeks. So did glasses of Chianti.

"You're very quiet," I said.

"Anxious," she said. "The Feng Yups are making their power known."

"Worse than the Sam Yups?"

"I think worse."

We both ordered ravioli, whose rich scent filled the room—the small pasta squares filled with sausage, brains, parsley, and spinach, and coated with a gravy spiced with herbs.

"Tell me what you know of Jabez Stone," I said.

"He owned a small shipping company. I think there were

three or four ships. Trade with Shanghai and Canton. One of them broke up in a storm."

"Carrying girls?"

"I think it was westbound. There were other troubles. I believe there were financial difficulties."

"But his son left Harvard for other reasons."

Eliza nodded carefully.

"I've been aboard the *Oliver Ferris*. There is a rather impressive stateroom. The door locks from the outside."

Her eyes met mine. *"Oh, God!"* she whispered.

"There is also what seems to have been a photographic darkroom."

"I don't understand."

"Indecent photographs were taken and sold on the streets of San Francisco, four or five years ago. I think the young women were captives."

"Transported," Eliza said.

"What do you mean?"

"A two-way traffic. A triangular trade, like the old New England trade with China."

"White slavery."

"Yes."

"August Larkyn was a part of it."

"Yes," Eliza said, holding her cup up to her chin.

"You knew this?"

"I know it. It was before I came to San Francisco."

"You took your revolver to the party aboard the *Oriana* when Larkyn was shot. To threaten him."

"Isabella da Costa had come to me for advice. She wished to be a music hall entertainer. August Larkyn had offered to assist her. But he insisted that she come alone to the *Oriana* so that photographs could be made. I knew very well what his intentions were. I was going to tell him I would kill him if he tried to corrupt that precious young woman."

"As he had her predecessor."

"I don't know about that," she said firmly. "Did he?"

"I think he recruited young women for that locked room aboard the *Oliver Ferris.*"

I saw the glint of tears in her eyes.

"And now the son is trying to take on his father's role."

"It may be that he is, Tom."

We finished our pasta in silence. The last of the wine was poured, coffee ordered.

Looking down at her pale, square, ringless hands, Eliza said, "Did you come to visit me that first time at the Mission because of Father Flanagan?"

"He sent me to you because of the piece I had written on the slave girls."

"I called on him at Old St. Mary's yesterday. He is such a sweet man. His face and manner are full of forgiveness."

I sipped coffee pretending my heart was not beating fast. I cleared my throat. "May I ask why you called on him?"

"Why, for forgiveness, of course!" she said, and laughed.

———

In my room there was the usual prudish fuss about disrobing, for she could not bear to be seen naked. She usually left a nightgown in my closet for these nights, but had taken it off to the laundry and not brought it back. I lay in bed in the pitchy dark listening in a vast excitement to the rustle of her clothing as it was discarded, and at last she slipped in beside me with one electric hand touching my shoulder.

I thought my mother would be very pleased by her.

———

The window was a rectangle of gray dawn when I rose for a morning micturition. Returning, I halted inside the door to admire my bride-to-be. She was sprawled gracefully beneath a tangle of coverlets, her hair spread over one cheek and her other pressed against her folded hands on the pillow. One pink-toed foot protruded from the blankets, a long pale leg, a lovely hemisphere of hip fairing into the ivory small of her back. I watched her long, naked body almost breathlessly, for she was as perfect as Tessie Powers, startlingly perfect, longer-limbed, ivory white. In the stillness of the room I could hear the faint murmur of her breathing.

With a shrug of her shoulders she changed position. The other buttock was revealed, It seemed to be stained with something, and I leaned closer to see that it was a tattoo, and I leaned closer still to read the words. I could hear the sound of my own breathing as I made out what it was:

F S I will love
you till I die

I leaned over farther to fold a corner of the bedclothes to cover the tattoo, and vowed to myself that she would never know that I had seen it. I crept back into bed with a weight of iron on my chest.

CHAPTER SEVENTEEN

ADORE, v.t. To venerate expectantly.
— *The Devil's Dictionary*

SATURDAY, MAY 29, 1891

Implosions of jealous fury at Frank Stone in all his ramifications would crash into my mood, and be fought off, and reassault me, as Eliza and I had a breakfast on the corner: scrambled eggs, sweet fritters, and coffee. I had planned to speak of marriage this morning, but I did not.

I accompanied Eliza to the Stockton Street Mission, where a young Chinese man in Western clothing awaited her. I was introduced to Wing Wo, who would be lawyering for the Mission in the place of the late attorney Duggan.

"Mr. Duggan trained Wing Wo himself!" Eliza said proudly. "Wing Wo studied in his office for two years. And accompanied him in court on occasion."

"I was in court with Mr. Duggan three times!" Wing Wo said in good English, holding up three fingers. He had a smooth round face, as pale as Eliza's. "Twice I spoke before the judge!"

"You speak very well," I said.

"Thank you, Mr. Redmond. I have had good help from Miss Lindley and Miss Cochran."

"Wing Wo has asked for Fah Loo's hand in marriage," Eliza

said, smiling pink-cheeked. "All of us here are holding our breath awaiting her answer."

"I am holding breath most of all!" Wing Ho said, bowing.

"It is the spring season that brings thoughts of marriage," Eliza said.

We all laughed dutifully.

————

Late in the morning a messenger delivered a familiar blue folded sheet of paper in a matching envelope to me in my cubicle at the *Examiner,* a missive from Eliza. I gazed on it with misgivings before I opened it:

> *TR, I have to entrain for Sacramento. I don't know when I'll be back, I hope tomorrow. EL*

The initials did not improve my mood. Nor had I been asked to accompany her in my role as writer for Annie Laurie's rewrite, and as Eliza's protector.

The fact that Bierce was working on some unspecified project for Willie Hearst meant that he needed no special word from the editors to detach me from regular duties to be his project-partner. Today's first labors consisted of examining the postcards which Mammy Pleasant had brought him. There were six of these, semi-naked girls in various poses that were more embarrassing than stimulating. One of the girls, with a lush figure, wore the same Moroccan half-veil as in the photographs in Captain Larkyn's collection; two others were of the same girl—in one, revealingly unwrapped in the Stars and Stripes, in the other, bent back bare-breasted, lips to a trumpet aimed at the top of the card. It was Bierce's intention to show the cards to Captain Chandler of the Detective Bureau to see if the faces matched those of any of San Francisco's missing young women.

"Seduced by Larkyn into having photographs made aboard Jabez Stone's *Oliver Ferris*," I said. "Made captive there in whatever horrible circumstance and usages I can't even bear to consider. And then what?"

"Some of them did not return to their daily lives," Bierce said grimly.

"Frank Stone may have been in communication with Larkyn to resume this trade."

"That is only a guess."

"Larkyn had Isabella da Costa in his web, the queen of next week's Fcsta."

"Regard this," Bierce said, and passed me a seventh photograph. This was a very different image, a man and a woman coupling, her white knees raised on either side of his naked buttocks, an arm concealing her face. The man was corpulent, and most shocking was the helmet mask he wore, the same that I had found in the bureau drawer aboard the *Oliver Ferris;* the prominent beak, the cock's comb, a slot below the beak for the eyes, the whole ugly head raised and thrown back as though crowing in a triumph of humiliation and degradation.

"My God!" I said.

"Yes."

I handed back the evil photograph.

Bierce passed the palm of his hand over the chalky brow of the skull on his desk, as though for luck. He said, "We come to the essential question in all these matters. Why was the deed done? And why was the deed done at its particular moment?"

I couldn't get that evil cock's head out of my mind's eye. "The deed was done to avenge the corruption and maybe murder of young women, and to prevent it happening again."

"In the general case, or the specific?" he asked.

"In the general case of young women who had the vulnerability of wanting to become theatrical performers, and specifically Miss da Costa."

"Or the deed was done to prevent young Mr. Stone and Captain Larkyn from setting up the same diabolical combination that had existed with Larkyn and the elder Stone."

And then he said, "But poor Billings was murdered on the mistaken belief that he was party to the photographing of the kidnapped young women. If it were not for that, Tom, one could abandon the murder of Larkyn as well warranted."

I watched him put the rooster-head photograph away in his drawer, separately from the others.

———

Winnie Sweet was announced by the sharp rap of heels in the hallway, and she swung into Bierce's office, white shirtwaist, long black skirt that swished past the door frame, vivid head of hair, a necklace of red stones to match it at her throat.

"Brosy! Hello, Tom."

"Good morning, Winnie."

Bierce, rising from behind his desk, was transparently pleased to see her. She patted the skull's cranium and smiled at him.

"I read your stories last night," she said to him. "They are wonderful, Brosy! Don't you think they are wonderful, Tom?"

"I do." I did, with reservations.

"But Brosy, the pretty young women never *do* appear!" It had been Petey McEwen's criticism.

"Ah, Winnie, I was not concerned with pretty young women appearing."

"But I know you are interested in young women appearing, because you have assured me you are pleased when I come here to harangue you! He has, you know, Tom," she said to me.

"What do you harangue him about, Winnie?"

"Oh, the Little Jim party I am planning."

"Now we are in for it, Tom," Bierce said.

I knew Bierce was quite taken with Winnie Sweet, who was now pacing before his desk, showing off her figure, I thought. I had never seen him with his cynical guard down before, and it bothered me like a smudge on the national banner.

Like me, Winnie was concerned with changing the botch-work world. Now she went to the window and leaned forward to gaze down at Montgomery Street, revealing pleasing curves.

"I can't see him from here," she said. "But he is down there.

"I will do all the work," she continued, turning back. "I'll do an Annie Laurie on it. But Brosy, you must submit to being the Grand Bashaw."

"No, I will not!" Bierce said.

"Oh, Brosy, please! It will be so fine if you will preside. Everyone will come."

"I have a position and a reputation to protect, my dear."

"Can you help, Tom?"

"They would run him out of the Cynics' Party," I said.

"Oh, it's just so silly. It would be such a grand event. Sam won't be half as good at it, Brosy."

"You just see if Sam will put up fifty dollars, and I'll match it. Instead."

"I *knew* that's what you'd say! But I just don't want to do it that way. I want people to be interested. This poor little fellow, no mother—his mother was a plain prostitute, you know. Who could possibly know who his father was? Dragging his poor leg around. He has a chance to be a proper healthy person, Dr. Jenks says, and I'm going to see that he has that chance!" She jammed her fists onto her hips and glared at Bierce.

"You are very handsome when you are in your fiery mood, my dear," Bierce said.

"Join me! Wouldn't he be fine, presiding over an event like this, Tom?"

"Fine," I said. "But out of character."

"Oh, pooh, out of character! We know there is a sweet person inside Bitter Bierce, don't we?"

Bierce said, "If I did it this one time I would have to go on doing it forever. Now I can say that I just don't perform monkeyshines like this, my dear. And I have a history that proves it."

But I thought she had him, and she gave me a twitch of a smile so that I knew she knew it too.

"And how is the indomitable Miss Lindley?" she said to me.

"I have a note that she's gone off to Sacramento."

Her smile vanished. "By herself? She shouldn't do that! I'm afraid they will lay a trap for her there!"

"She is the indomitable Miss Lindley," I said.

I excused myself to go back to my cubicle, and Winnie presently popped in there. She did not parade herself so provocatively with me as she did with Bierce, which could mean she was not interested in me in that way, or that she knew I was beguiled by Eliza Lindley.

"He'll do it, don't you think?" she said.

"I think you know how to get him to do it."

"I was very disturbed by the stories in his *Soldiers and Civilians,* Tom. They are all about death! Does he think about death so much?"

"He had terrible experiences in the war. Of course they have marked his writing."

"He never speaks of the war to me."

"He writes of it, as you now know."

"I do know. Too much, I think. He is not a happy man, Tom."

"He is a serious man, Winnie. He is serious about writing, about his stories, and the fables he's been writing lately, and even 'Prattle,' I think. And if his stories are about death they are serious, aren't they?"

"He criticizes my writing. He criticizes it quite cruelly! But I write about serious things too. Little Jim is a serious thing. He is a child and he's suffering! Ambrose should be concerned."

"We both know he will, in the end, preside at your function," I said.

"I'm afraid he will just do it because he likes me, not for Little Jim."

"But perhaps he likes you because you care about the Little Jims."

She thought about that, standing with one fist on one hip, and one boot cocked. "That's nice, Tom," she said. "Thank you!" She spun around to head out the door, but stopped and turned back.

"He makes fun of me," she said, "but I think he likes me!" She gave me a dazzling smile. It vanished and her face became serious.

"You are his friend," she said.

"Yes."

"You know how he feels about marriage."

"We have both heard him on the subject."

"He has suggested another arrangement."

"Like Willie and Tessie?"

Her face had reddened. "I cannot do that, Tom."

"He is married, you know. He and Mrs. Bierce are separated merely."

"I like him very much," Winnie Sweet said. "But I can't do that. I was not brought up that way."

"I'm sure you were not," I said.

This time she smiled sadly before she departed with her quick rap of heels.

I thought of my own situation, and Eliza's, and it seemed I had prevailed in some kind of competition I did not even want to think about.

————

In the morning, again, a dead rat lay just outside my door, bloody nose, hairless tail, birdlike claws folded, and this time I knew it was a warning or a response to the Annie Laurie piece on the Sacramento rescue, or else to Eliza Lindley's frequent presence in my rooms.

This time I did not call Mr. Barker to remove the corpse, but gingerly wrapped it in yesterday's *Examiner* and carried it down Sacramento Street to deposit it in an ash can.

CHAPTER EIGHTEEN

DELUSION, n. The father of a most respectable family, comprising Enthusiasm, Affection, Self-denial, Faith, Hope, Charity, and many other goodly sons and daughters.

— The Devil's Dictionary

SUNDAY, MAY 30, 1891

I played well enough to be pleased with myself in the Firemen versus Police game on Sunday morning, with two base hits and a gee-whiz double play in which I had the pleasure of throwing out at first a detective acquaintance of mine, Barney Phelps. To the sorrow of the Firemen, however, the Police won the game 6–5. We were not having a good spring.

After the game, when Barney and I sat on a bench together to talk a few things over, he said, "You and Mr. Bierce looking into some missing women, I understand."

"With not much cooperation from Captain Chandler, I understand."

"After what Almighty God Bierce did to Captain Pusey? Ran him right out of town."

"Someone could point out to Captain Chandler that he wouldn't be chief of detectives if Pusey hadn't been run out of town for blackmail and a pack of felonies never prosecuted."

"Not for me to do, Tom. I'll point out to you, though, that the chief don't have any great regard for seeing his name in 'Prattle.'"

"Reward for unworth," I said.

"What's this about disappeared women?"

"Young women from the City riding the ferries over to Sausalito to the grand parties on the British yachts anchored there. Some disappeared."

"If they disappeared in Sausalito that's Chief Casey's to-do."

"No one knows just where they disappeared. They were young ladies from San Francisco."

"I don't think the chief wants anything to do with anything Mr. Bierce has to do with."

"If you could hunt me up a list of names."

"Why don't Chief Casey put in to Chandler for it?"

I said I would see to that, if he had not done so already.

When I got back to my rooms there was a message from Bierce that I should take a ferry to Sausalito immediately; Captain Larkyn's mate had turned up in the bay.

The message was peremptory in tone. Bierce did not have much sympathy for my pursuit of excellence on the ball field.

And the fourth shoe had fallen.

———

The drowned body of Jack Croft lay on a table in the back room of the Delphinium Saloon on Sausalito's main street— scrawny, bald as an egg, and gray-faced; dragged out of the bay this morning. I remembered him as a man of some size, but now he looked no bigger than a twelve-year-old boy. He had apparently fallen off the *Oriana* and taken a crack on the head in the process, or—just as likely, according to Chief Casey, who stood with us to view the body—he had taken a crack on the head and then gone into the bay.

"Wasn't as unholy bad as Larkyn, but he was scamp enough," the chief said.

"He was certainly aware of what went on in Larkyn's state-room," Bierce said. "I have no doubt he was an accomplice."

"If this keeps up, the British fleet is going to move on to somewheres where they are not getting shot or knocked on the head for their sins."

"Might not some locals be relieved at that?"

"Storekeepers and saloons like this one would suffer. The good-folks Brits would be relieved enough."

"Surely this is connected with Larkyn and Billings."

Chief Casey made a cheek-sucking sound. "Reckon so," he said.

"There were other yachtsmen with Larkyn's morals," Bierce said.

"Captain Bastable, anyway. I'll be hearing from him, no doubt."

I moved around the table for a better view of Croft. A pair of mismatched coins had been laid in his eye sockets. He had taken a severe whack on his right temple, just at the hairline, with broken skin and bruising there. He had lobsterlike hands half-clenched into fists.

"Jasper Billings," Bierce said.

"He don't fit in, do he? Just, he was a photographer and there is photygraphs in it."

"There were photographs circulated of unclothed young ladies," Bierce said. "I have a half-dozen in my possession, and one is quite troubling. I believe some of the subjects were women who had come over from the City for festivities on the yachts, and then disappeared."

The chief blew out his breath again. "Is that so, Mr. Bierce?"

"I'm afraid it is, Chief Casey. It would be well if you would get in touch with Captain Chandler in the City in regard to these disappearances."

Casey did not look pleased at the prospect, but nodded in agreement.

Bierce related to him all that we knew, or had surmised.

He moved around the table to survey the corpse from different angles. "Anybody know anything about this?" he asked.

"Only one fellow aboard at the time, new crewman name of Coffey. He went to sleep early after an evening ashore, probably whiffled. Didn't hear anything unusual. Then in the morning Croft was gone, and the dory still tied up. Coffey come in to me when he got around to it, but by then one of the Portygees had spotted the floater. The coroner's going to reason out he fell and smacked his head and went over the side."

"Another accident like Billings's," I said.

"I guess that is what I'll report, 'less I get something else to go on," Casey said. "It'd be a bit too bad if the Englishers packed up and set sail for Hawaii or somewheres."

He covered Croft's body with the sheet. The mate was not much of a presence beneath it.

———

We followed the chief in drifting fog back to his office, which was above a pharmacy on the main street. A window with a bellying curtain was open on the dock side, and a water's edge stink of fish drifted in from the rotting piles along the docks. There was a small, neat desk and some straight chairs.

We had not had time to seat ourselves when a fat yachtsman in a blue jacket with brass buttons barged inside. He had a walrus moustache, disordered hair, pouched blue eyes, and a redolence of whiskey about him.

"See here, Casey!"

"Good morning, Captain Bastable. These here is Mr. Bierce and Mr. Redmond. Captain Bastable."

"It is another murder, sir. I will notify the British Consul in the City!"

"Good idea," Casey said, and folded his arms.

"They are dead set after British subjects, clearly. Whoever they are, gang of wogs, probably. Come aboard your yacht, shoot you, or knock you on the head. Who is next, sir?"

Bastable had a considerable corporation behind the blue serge and brass buttons, which he maneuvered around the small room like a sack of potatoes. I didn't think he would be able to pass through an ordinary doorway broadside.

"Portuguese, do you think, Captain?" Bierce said.

Bastable switched his belly around so as to peer at Bierce. "Who are you, sir?"

"As Chief Casey just pointed out, my name is Bierce. I am a journalist connected with the San Francisco *Examiner*. Mr. Redmond is my assistant."

"Filthy sheet," Bastable said, not unpleasantly.

"We do our best, Captain," Bierce said. "I repeat myself: do you think Portuguese are responsible?"

Bastable said, "They are poor and the British subjects here are rich by their standards; stands to reason there is class jealousy. Of course they are to be suspected. Any fool could see that!"

"I don't think robbery has been a motivation in these events," Bierce said.

"This fellow seems remarkably opinionated for an outsider, Chief Casey!"

"He is investigating the murders here for the *Examiner*."

"My God, next thing we will all be smeared over the front page of that garbage wrap! Just leave me out of it! That's the word with the bark on it, sir!"

I thought it better not to say it sounded like the bark merely. Bierce seated himself and crossed his legs, hat on his lap.

Bastable shoved his corporation toward Casey. "I have stood by while there has been absolutely no progress on poor Augie's murder," he said. "I will not stand idly by this time! This matter is to be pursued with full rigor, do you understand me, sir?"

Casey held his peace, and nodded.

"We can weigh anchor and leave this beastly hole in about three days time, sir, and do not think we are not considering a move to somewhere where we will be treated with the consideration we demand. San Diego! There is a splendid harbor there, splendid climate, fine little city. Three days' steam, sir."

"That'd be about right," Casey said, still standing facing Captain Bastable.

"We are aware of Captain Larkyn's sideline," Bierce said suddenly. I thought he had probably suffered some gorge rise from the fat yachtsman.

Bastable shifted his sack of potatoes. "What the devil do you mean, sir?"

"Mr. Redmond and I came over here because we had heard the British yachtsmen here referred to as one-eyed jacks, and we wished to discover what that could mean. Captain Larkyn has illustrated the meaning."

"August Larkyn was my old friend, sir. I will not listen to scurrilous—"

"That too is well known," Bierce interrupted.

Bastable's face turned scarlet.

"It appears," Bierce said, "that Captain Larkyn was involved in schemes to seduce and kidnap young women, and perhaps sell them into a vile slavery. That he was also involved in the making of pornographic photographs, and perhaps in league with Chinese merchants in slave girls, and perhaps in murder. One can only assume Croft was in league with him. In fact, the world is a considerably better place with Captain Larkyn and his mate gone to their eternal and highly caloric rest."

"By God, sir—" Bastable cried out. "That is *Examiner* filth announced at the source! Chief Casey, you allow these lies to be uttered in your office?"

"Well, I don't know for sure," Casey said. "But there may be some truth in it."

"This will be reported to the British Consul, sir!"

"Good idea," Casey said again, nodding.

"By God, sir," Bastable said. "I suppose this mongrel nation has no laws prohibiting libels against gentlemen. August Larkyn was descended from one of the most prominent families in Suffolk, sir!"

His face bloomed with tiny bright veins, but I thought he was not angry, he was scared; and I thought he would indeed weigh anchor in something less than three days' time.

"If you wouldn't mind answering a few questions about the activities of August Larkyn—" Bierce said.

"I will not!" Captain Bastable almost shouted. "And good day to you, Chief." He slammed out. His heavy footsteps in the hall shook the building.

"As a matter of fact, I believe San Diego's gain won't be much of a loss," Chief Casey said calmly enough.

———

A fable in "Prattle":

THE PENITENT THIEF

A Boy who had been taught by his Mother to steal grew to be a man and was a professional public official. One day he was taken in the act and condemned to die. While going to the place of execution he passed his Mother and said to her:

"Behold your work! If you had not taught me to steal I should not have come to this."

"Indeed!" said the Mother. "And who, pray, taught you to be detected?"

CHAPTER NINETEEN

JUSTICE, n. A commodity which in more or less adulterated condition the State sells to the citizen as a reward for his allegiance, taxes and personal service.

— The Devil's Dictionary

TUESDAY, JUNE 1, 1891

Eliza's friend Matt Fenton knocked on my door Tuesday morning before eight o'clock. His white spike of beard jerked as he spoke.

"You haven't heard from her, have you, Redmond?"

"Just that she was taking the train to Sacramento."

"A friend in Sacramento telephoned to say she is in court today there, charged with kidnapping. Can you do anything?"

I telephoned my father from Sam Chamberlain's office at the *Examiner.* He knew a lawyer who could get a continuance at least.

I caught a ferry across the bay, and the SP in Oakland, bound for Sacramento.

———

There were no hacks free at the depot in Sacramento, so I trotted the four blocks to my parents' house toting my valise. The parlor was alight with a new electric lamp. Seated were four people—my father and mother, Eliza and a fat, bald-headed man with a neckless head, chin resting on his chest—the room in a pall of cigar smoke. My mother leaped up to embrace me.

I shook hands with my father; Eliza hung back, looking tired and maybe scared, in a tight jacket and a blouse with a soiled white collar.

"I'm so glad you've come, Tom," she said in a low voice.

When we were married and I had some rightful say in her activities, she would involve herself in something less dangerous than child rescue, such as child rearing.

The fat man, who didn't bother to disengage his bulk from the rocker, was an attorney, Mr. Horace Ellery.

"Continuance till tomorrow," my father the Gent said, standing straddle-legged and pleased with himself before the coal grate.

My mother held my hands and looked into my face with her sweet smile, her blue eyes aproned with dark flesh like raccoon eyes.

"I was just saying the little lady here surely walked into one," Ellery said.

"Is that so?"

"They was primed and ready for her, yes sir," Ellery said. "Had all the toast buttered, looks to me. Note for her to come up here on a rescue business, and they switched chillun on her, so she collared the legitimate daughter. Police on the ready. Shysters on hand. Oh, they are a sweet bunch, they are."

"Frank Stone has offered to put up my bail," Eliza said to me.

"He's here?"

She shook her head. "But he's part of it."

"How serious is this?" I asked Ellery, who had propped an unlit cigar in his jaw.

"Be serious if they got away with it, young fellow. They are not going to get away with it."

My mother asked if anyone wanted coffee. My father offered whiskey. Eliza asked for coffee. My mother fussed over her no doubt as a prospective daughter-in-law and grandchild-producer to a degree that made me nervous.

My father agitated his eyebrows at me, to convey that Ellery, being a Sacramentan and probably connected with the SP railroad, was the best in the business.

"We will just jack up some fresh evidence for Judge Briscoe," Ellery said. He was now working himself from side to side and I saw that he was shedding the chair like a chrysalis. I didn't know how to help him.

"Redmond," he said, grabbing the hand my father extended to help him up. "I'm going to make some rounds, scratch together some witnesses. See you in court. So long, now, Mrs. Redmond. You show up, now, Miss Lindley, or I'm in the soup."

"I will, Mr. Ellery!" Eliza said. "And I can't thank you enough."

"Never mind that, never mind that," Ellery said, and, collecting his hat and shifting his great weight from one leg to the other, made his ponderous way toward the door. His very heft was confidence-inspiring.

"Best in the business," my father whispered.

When my mother handed Eliza the cup and saucer, I heard the rattle of porcelain; so Eliza was not so cool as she pretended. The Gent held up his whiskey glass in a toast.

"Here's to whatever knavery it is that will set you free tomorrow, Miss Lindley," he said.

We sipped our various libations to that thought.

"Have you jumped in the Bay any more lately, Tommy?" my mother wanted to know.

———

The courtroom was empty except for a uniformed constable when the three of us arrived, Judge Briscoe not on the bench yet. But presently a bearded attorney entered with a big flashy Asian gent in flowing red-and-yellow silk robes and a black skullcap, who glared at Eliza. Eliza glared back, arms folded under her bosom.

Horace Ellery lumbered in, also with a Chinese in tow. This was a skinny, sallow little fellow dressed in a black suit and vest. Big flashy, Eliza's enemy, did not appear pleased to see him; he and the attorney whispered together. Ellery beamed at us.

Now the judge appeared, full-bearded, and climbed to the bench. A stout patrolman had accompanied him.

"Your Honor," Ellery said. "I do believe our opponents here are about to withdraw charges."

"Is this true, Mr. Mack?" the judge asked in a hard voice.

"My client and I are conferring on the matter," the lean lawyer said. He and his flashy client conferred. The skinny Chinese stood watching them with his fingers knitted together before his chest. I thought the judge winked at Horace Ellery, who stood facing him sturdy as a fireplug. Eliza had seated herself, straight-backed, to observe the proceedings.

"Ha!" my father muttered under his breath, as suddenly the flashy Chinese swung around in a swirl of red and yellow and stalked out.

Our man watched him go expressionlessly. The lean attorney, Mack, bowed to the judge.

"Dismissed!" the judge said. "You are a free woman, Miss Lindley. But let me warn you in the future to confine your well-known escapades to the City of San Francisco!"

"Thank you, Your Honor," Eliza said, rising.

———

Back at my parents' house there was a telegram from Bierce: "Tom, Mrs. Pleasant says to look into an entertainer named Glory Starr at a music hall there called the Bird Cage. AGB."

My father knew the Bird Cage well, and had seen Miss Starr in song and dance—"A very lively young woman," he pronounced her. I thought she must be one of the missing females. Eliza begged off a music hall evening, but accepted my mother's invitation to spend the night; she and I would take the *Delta Queen* back down the river to San Francisco in the morning. I had scarcely had an occasion to be alone with her.

———

The Bird Cage on its side street was a jewel of electric light, a shadowy facade beneath a broad balcony strung with light-bulbs, sounds of music, and a large billboard depicting a female showing plump stockinged legs beneath draped red and white stripes, a head of red hair, and a blue-and-stars head-dress, in a gallant pose:

GLORY STARR AT THE BIRD CAGE

My father had to greet the usual number of other gents, both distinguished with plug hats and undistinguished with cloth caps, more than one of both categories fragrant with whiskey. My father passed a coin to one who looked down on his luck. He was in a festive mood. He seemed proud to introduce me as his "journalist son from the City." Tickets were a dollar apiece.

We sat in the best seats, below the stage, in a mounting racket of shuffling boots and conversations as the Bird Cage filled—seats in front, stalls a level higher, men and women, heat from the lights, reek of perspiration, for it was hot in Sacramento unless it was cold. A five-piece band of music assembled just in front of us, clad in yellow trousers and white shirts, with blooming red bow ties. They sawed and tooted for a time.

First up was a comedian with a tangled yellow wig and a cravat, the end of which protruded from his pant leg. He made comedy stepping over and around this, and told jokes that my father found hilarious.

Then Glory Starr appeared in the costume from the billboard, a pretty redhead in her red-and-white-striped flowing skirt, a blue, white-starred blouse, and cap. She cavorted. "Ah, what a lovely piece!" my father almost groaned. The band of music played a medley of Civil War songs, and she halted her dance to stand at attention, a hand raised to her brow in salute. She sang in a pleasant soprano voice. When the familiar songs continued, she danced to them, running this way and that, flinging her limbs about in a revealing manner. She had a heart-shaped face, dark eyes, a reddened mouth, powdered face and arms. She left the stage to wild applause, returned for another song, left to another ovation.

"Well," my father said, "is she one of your missing young women?"

I had no idea; Miss Rogers, Miss Kelly, or another? "Can you arrange for us to meet with her after the show?"

He could. Her dressing room was small and crowded, heaps of clothing and costumes hanging off hooks on the wall. Miss Starr sat at a dressing table facing a mirror, and, when she had greeted us, turned back to her reflected features. She dabbed at her face with a napkin, and made a gesture with her other hand apologizing that there was nowhere to sit.

She asked our business in her chirpy voice.

I identified myself, and said the San Francisco *Examiner* was investigating murders in Sausalito, and I'd been notified she might be able to furnish some information.

"About who?" she said.

"August Larkyn and his mate Jack Croft. And Jasper Billings."

She scrunched her face at the mirror again. "Augie Larkyn

offered to get me a position in the profession that interested me. But there was a price I didn't want to pay."

"Photographs?" I said.

"Oh, yes!"

"Other things?"

"Of course. I declined. I got my own position, and it took some doing, but I got it myself, and I am making a good living, thank you."

"Famous all over Sacramento," my father said.

"And in Auburn and Colfax!" Glory Starr said with a laugh.

"There are missing young women we are looking for who had to do with Larkyn. May I ask who you are?"

She shook her head. "I have no past."

But of course with her dyed red hair and her dark eyes, she was Flora Rodrigues, who was dead insofar as her mother was concerned, but not to her father. I felt an enormous relief.

"Your secret is safe with me," I said, and her eyes switched from the mirror to my face.

"Augie Larkyn, and that fat toad Bastable, and another dastardly fellow—"

"Jabez Stone."

"Wanted me to take my clothes off so they could have a look, but there was no point in it because you felt them looking right through your clothes anyhow."

"The *Oliver Ferris,*" I said.

She looked puzzled and shook her head.

"It was a ship where they had a place to take photographs and a darkroom setup."

She shook her head again. "It was to be just on Augie's yacht—what was it? *Oriana.* Not buck naked, some filmy garments—he showed them to me. It would be a great help in assisting me in getting work in the City. I left with my honor

172 • Oakley Hall

intact, gentlemen. But you know, it made me determined to—go out on my own. So I ups and lefts, and it was rocky and then it was just fine."

"The queen who disappeared," I said.

Her face tightened differently, her eyes were hard. "You know," she said.

"Your secret is safe with me," I said again.

"But you are a newspaperman working for that dreadful newspaper."

"On my honor."

"Let me tell you something, Mister Newspaperman," she said. "I had a friend from San Francisco that got mixed up with Captain Larkyn. Betty Samuels, her name was. What happened to her? That's what I want to know. Just all at once she was gone off the planet. And that was when I decided I didn't want anything more to to with Captain Larkyn."

"He's dead," I said. "So is Croft."

She crossed herself.

"You certainly do put on a fine show, little lady," my father said.

"Thank you, sir!"

A man with slicked-down hair and a fancy moustache stuck his head in the door. "These gents bothering you, Miss Starr?"

"They are just leaving," Flora Rodrigues said, turning back to the mirror again.

———

At home my mother was distressed because Eliza had changed her mind and decided to take a room at a hotel downtown; nothing she could do. About two hours ago.

"What a forthright and courageous young lady she is!" my mother said. "And very handsome!"

"I love her very much," I said.

My mother laid a hand over her mouth and stared at me with her heart in her eyes.

"I believe she is taking instruction from Father Flanagan, though she has not said so."

"I so would like a grandchild before I get any older," my mother said.

"You'll have to get a *little* older, the way I understand it," my father said jovially.

I told them I would be taking the milk train in the morning.

THURSDAY, JUNE 3, 1891

At the depot, in gray first light, indistinct figures moved against the shuttered ticket windows, a woman in a deep bonnet, a small girl with her face similarly concealed, hands clasped together. Eliza had gone back to the rescue.

Face on, her features were drawn with tension. "Oh, Tom," she said in a tone of relief.

"May I join you?"

"Oh, yes!"

The train chuffed into the station, conductor standing on a step. If he was the same one who had carried Eliza to safety as related by Annie Laurie, he did not recognize her.

"Early birds!" he said. I assisted Eliza and her charge to board. A few men slept on the green plush seats in the dimness of the carriage. Eliza and I seated ourselves with the silent Chinese child between us.

It seemed an age before the train came to life and gathering speed, chuffed on out of the Sacramento station. Eliza sank back in her seat with a sigh.

The child pointed silently at fields as we passed them, trees in clumps like misty bouquets, a white farmhouse catching a splash of sunlight.

"All right, now!" Eliza whispered. She tittered nervously. "The conductor must think we are a married couple with our child! How would your mother like this grandchild, Tom?"

I said I didn't think it was what my mother had in mind.

"We will just have to make one ourselves."

"Will you marry me first?" I asked.

"Of course I will!"

Our child stood up on our seat, peering out the windows at the dawn landscapes from under her bonnet, sometimes pointing silently. Eliza's hand clutched mine. I could ignore the tattoo, couldn't I?

Thus we returned to San Francisco.

CHAPTER TWENTY

MAN, n. An animal so lost in rapturous contemplation of what he thinks he is as to overlook what he indubitably ought to be.
— *The Devil's Dictionary*

FRIDAY, JUNE 4, 1891

The office of Sam Chamberlain looked down busy Montgomery Street on the roofs of carriages, buggies and drays, and streetcars moving in slow peristalsis north and south. Sam wore a pin-striped suit with a flowered lapel, his monocle swinging from its cord. He and Bierce stood together at the window, Sam pointing out something on the street below. Winnie Sweet sat in a chair opposite me, legs crossed, notebook gripped on her lap, red hair stacked above her vivid, pretty face. We were waiting for William Randolph Hearst, Proprietor and Publisher.

Bierce seated himself. Sam sighed and turned from the window. He said, "Winnie, what about this second Sacramento adventure of Miss Lindley's?"

"I'm working on a piece on Little Jim, but I'll get to it if Tom will rough it out."

"It is time to give Miss Lindley's adventures a rest," I said.

"Why is that, Tom?"

"This is the second time they've tried to ambush her. There's also some question about lawyer Duggan's death. Did he fall or was he pushed?"

"We'll see what Mr. Hearst says," Sam said.

Bierce had his knitted-brow look of disapproval: "There is an involvement on his part."

"How is that?" Sam asked.

"Tessie."

Sam shook his head, puzzled.

"A fellow who offered to pay Miss Lindley's bail in Sacramento is the son of old Jabez Stone. He has a certain position with the Feng Yups because his father owned the *Oliver Ferris,* which was in the very lucrative trade of importing girl slaves. The son was at Harvard with Willie."

"Why would he offer to pay her bail?" Sam inquired.

"Another ambush," I said.

Winnie wrote, a corner of her tongue appearing between her red lips. "Can we get all this in, Tom?"

"As I say, I think we must let Miss Lindley retire from the front page for a while."

Bierce continued: "Frank Stone operated a salon of prostitutes for the undergraduates at Harvard. He was asked not to return there for that reason. Tessie was probably connected to the enterprise."

Sam whistled softly. Winnie closed her notebook.

"I prophesy," Bierce said, "that Willie will have been, or will be, subject to an attempt to blackmail him to save Tessie's reputation."

"What reputation is there to save?" Sam inquired.

"There are always darker regions to be plumbed."

"Miss Powers is worth more than her reputation!" Winnie said forcefully.

Bierce frowned at her. "Women are usually quicker to attack personal failure among their gender than men."

"Many of us know just how easy it is to take the primrose path," Winnie said, with a sideways glance at me.

Sam said, "So your position, Ambrose, is that Willie is vulnerable in a blackmail situation. Are the Sausalito murders involved?"

"They are."

"May I ask how the investigation is proceeding?"

"It is, in effect, finished."

"You know the assassin, then?"

"I am not ready to produce him."

"Is this because of Willie's vulnerability?"

"It is in part."

"The gee-whiz story is what we are here for, as we all know," Sam said. He removed his monocle, and flipped it on the end of its string.

"Mysterious doings and undoings!" Winnie said in her pert voice.

"I wonder," Sam said, "if Mr. Hearst won't say damn the torpedoes, full speed ahead."

"It may be well to consider Mother Hearst," Bierce said, "who supplies the money that keeps this newspaper going. *She* would not say damn the torpedoes."

I reflected that the *Examiner,* which was often accused of making up its own facts, was also capable of leaving out inconvenient ones.

Willie Hearst's high voice was audible from the hallway.

"Winnie, if you please," Sam said.

Winnie rose, parceled out smiles, and departed.

"I'm afraid Winnie's concerns have settled upon Little Jim," Sam Chamberlain said.

"When aroused, she has the resolve of the maternal rhinoceros," Bierce said.

Willie Hearst bustled into the office.

"Mr. Chamberlain, Mr. Bierce, Mr. Redmond." He shook hands all around, and motioned everyone to sit. Tall, slim, straight-backed, he wore a blue-striped cravat and a high collar.

"So, Mr. Bierce, how are your and Mr. Redmond's investigations progressing?"

"I believe they should cease," Bierce said.

"Surely there is a story here, Mr. Bierce!"

"It may turn out not to be a story you like, Mr. Hearst."

"What does it matter, man, whether I like it or not?"

"It involves Frank Stone."

Willie turned to gaze out the window at the traffic on Montgomery Street. Sam Chamberlain had replaced his monocle.

"I will tell you something," Willie said, back to us. "Miss Powers has received a blackmail letter, and what would be a compromising photograph of herself in a nude state—if the photograph had not been so patently doctored."

"What did he want?" Bierce said.

"He wants the *Examiner* to cease its attacks on Chinatown principals. To cease attentions to the Feng Yups, the slave girls, the Stockton Street Mission, and attendant matters."

"Your mother was the recipient of a similar photograph."

"Yes, she has told me. There is another matter," Willie added. "There is a new steam launch on the bay. It has challenged the *Aquila* three times now. It is operated by Frank Stone, who was a classmate of mine at Harvard. He is close to having a faster boat. We know each other, and yet he will not acknowledge me. What does this mean?"

"It may have to do with Miss Powers," Bierce said.

Willie said nothing, still facing the window.

"And now another naval person in Sausalito has been murdered," Bierce said. "Larkyn's mate."

"Do you know the identity of the murderer, Mr. Bierce?" Willie demanded, swinging away from the window.

"I am not at this moment free to reveal it."

Willie's face was blotched with red. "What if I order you to reveal that identity to me now, Mr. Bierce?"

"I will deliver to you my resignation instead," Bierce said coolly.

Willie Hearst managed a smile. "We can't have that, can we? Very well, Mr. Bierce, you must manage this investigation as you see fit."

"I presumed those were my orders in the first place," Bierce said.

"The Miss Lindley articles will continue, Mr. Redmond?" Willie said.

"They must cease," I said.

Willie's face twisted violently. "Is this because of the blackmail attempt I have mentioned?"

"Because of it or not because of it, Miss Lindley is in danger. Miss Sweet may be, also, whose byline is on the articles."

"Well, then—" Willie said in a controlled voice. "I see that another cessation is imperative!"

He strode out of the office.

Sam Chamberlain made a dumb show of wiping sweat from his forehead. Bierce looked at me with a twist of his eyebrows.

"And when will you be presenting the grand revelation to us mere mortals, Ambrose?" Sam asked.

"Perhaps after the grand Festa of the Holy Ghost in Sausalito Sunday," Bierce said. "Or perhaps not at all."

"The front page of the *Examiner* breathlessly awaits your determinations."

"Thank you, Sam."

Bierce departed, leaving me with Sam Chamberlain.

"Almighty God Bierce," Sam said.

SATURDAY, JUNE 5, 1891

"Here is what Winnie has written," Bierce said the next day when I stopped by his office.

Little Jim's favorite seating location is on the curb on the southeast corner of Market and New Montgomery Streets. In his usual position, his crudely made crutch beside him, one leg is properly bent, but the other cannot bend because of some deep defect of bone and muscle which doctors believe may be corrected at great expense of their services and a bed in a hospital.

A bed is a luxury that Little Jim does not possess. He sleeps on a pile of rags in a doorway of an alley off 3rd Street, from which, however, he will probably be evicted soon, for the Irish sweeper in the alley has been giving him hard looks and muttering at him.

He is not sure how old he is. He thinks he may be eleven. He does not know his birthday. He has no mother or father, no relatives of any kind. His mother apparently worked in one of the Cow Yards south of Market. She is dead, he thinks, for he hasn't seen her for what must be a year, although he is uncertain as to time. Life was a little better for him when she was alive. He loved her.

Nevertheless, he has a sunny smile and cheerful greetings for the Market Street regulars who pass his post. No doubt readers of these words will have seen him there. He is small, and shy, but his hair is combed, his smile winning, and his crutch at the ready. Some of the passersby give him coins, some the remains of their sandwiches, a nice lady Tuesday gave him a whole apple. He remembers it because he has not had many whole apples.

Some months ago he was able to earn some coppers by carrying messages to guests in the Palace Hotel, painfully hauling himself and his stiffened leg up the stairs, bracing his progress with his crutch, because he was not allowed to use the elevator.

A person in a uniform with twelve brass buttons on the tunic told him he must not come into the Palace Hotel anymore. He is a little fragrant from being unwashed, and the guests' nasal passages might be offended, as well as their sight of this poor lad dragging his bad leg and his crutch up those wide staircases.

ANNIE LAURIE

"No doubt it will be well edited by Sam," Bierce said. "I am glad it is not my duty to do so."

"It will elicit some sympathy for this boy, and others like him," I said.

"That is all too clearly her intent," Bierce said stiffly. "Tomorrow is the Sausalito popery affair for which we have been waiting," he added. "I will meet you at the ten o'clock ferry."

So it was arranged.

————

The next morning there was another dead rat on my doorstep. This one's skull had been crushed, as though stamped on with a boot heel—brains, bone, and a little blood all over the step. Consequently I had to call Mr. Barker upstairs again.

He arrived in his overalls with sleeves rolled on his hairy arms. He squinted down at the dead rodent.

"You been trifling with the chinks, Mr. Redmond?"

"Why do you say that?"

"Things they do if you are in arrears over some fan-tan debts. Or opium. Or women. Maybe it's women."

I said I had no idea what it could be about.

I was in a shaky state when I met Bierce at the ferry, and I did not tell him of the third rat, as though it would be a confession of defect on my part.

CHAPTER TWENTY-ONE

CALAMITY, n. A more than commonly plain and unmistakable re-minder that the affairs of this life are not of our ordering. Calamities are of two kinds: misfortune to ourselves, and good fortune to others.
— *The Devil's Dictionary*

SUNDAY, JUNE 6, 1891

Sausalito was packed for the Festival of the Holy Ghost, which was a noncanonical lay celebration, as I understood it, although it coincided with the Pentecost. Smartly dressed crowds swarmed the streets, and herds of tan-and-white cattle decorated with chains and necklaces of flowers were driven along the esplanade by a cowboy with a cattle prod as long as a medieval lance. Lean-to stalls of poles strung over with green branches dispensed baked goods, wine in squads of dark bottles, fruit in colorful pyramids, decorated baskets, embroidery.

Clusters of little girls in white dresses, arms around each other, giggled together; women in their finery grouped in twos and threes; suited, hatted men formed larger assemblages, and arrayed themselves in shoulder-to-shoulder huddles at the wine lean-tos.

Older women's features had been turned harsh by their many pregnancies, men's from their ocean trade, but today all faces were smiling with greetings to friends and strangers. Celebratory men with weaving steps radiated friendship and wine fumes.

The street scenes did not much interest Bierce, and we turned into the Bon Ton Saloon, with its pleasant sawdust stench of red wine and beer.

Charles Peavine in a brass-buttoned blue jacket and sparkling white trousers looked in on us there, cap under his arm.

"Will you be coming to church with me, gents?" he asked. "It's a very colorful service, a solemn Grand Mass."

"I do not offend churches with my presence," Bierce said, in his most pompous tone.

"Tom?"

I said I would certainly accompany him.

———

Peavine explained to me that the Portuguese community's festival this Sunday was based on an event from thirteenth-century Portugal. Queen Isabel prayed to the Holy Ghost to end the famine that racked the country. Her prayers were answered. Thus a celebration of reenactment was held every year, a feast symbolic of the end of the famine and open to all, consisting of meat soup, bread, and wine following Mass, and a procession through the streets proclaiming a visit by the Holy Ghost. In the evening, with much gaiety, the celebrants danced an old Azorean dance called the Chama Rita. A young lady—the endangered Isabella da Costa this year, as I knew—represented Queen Isabel, wearing a crown that supported a white dove symbolizing the Holy Ghost. The event would begin in the Portuguese Hall in New Town and move from there, with a cart of bread to be blessed, to St. Mary Star of the Sea Church, where Mass would be celebrated and the Queen and Emperor crowned—after which all would troop back to the Portuguese Hall for the feast, and the dancing of the Chama Rita.

Peavine and I joined the press where the grand procession was assembling, everyone in Sunday best, black suits, white high-necked dresses, long capes extravagantly embroidered, flags, and banners depicting either the queen or the Virgin—perhaps both. Boys held up doves of fabric or papier-mâché. There was a cheerful racket and milling. Brass bands grew louder at intervals, then faded, to be replaced by others. All was noise and good fellowship. No one seemed in charge. The herd of cattle wended its dusty way along a parallel street. The cart of breads was in the form of a ship's hull. There was an overlay of the delicious fragrance of cooking meat.

"They say it is the perfume of heaven itself!" Peavine said, sniffing.

"Good smells and cheerful noise!" I said.

"Aye!"

"Good crowd!"

"When the Portuguese get crowded together like this they say, 'Too many Silvas!'" Peavine said. He and I became separated in the throngs before the church. Inside, I felt stirrings of pleasure and pride in my not very well maintained faith, in which I assumed my beloved intended to join me. My visions of her at my side were in another St. Mary's, at an altar less extravagant than this one.

St. Mary Star of the Sea was decorated in florid style, rich gleams of gold in a high-ceilinged and expansive dimness, icons and statues, above the altar a huge crucified Christ with realistic bloody knees and a bloody forehead from the thorns. Chapels decorated with branches and flowers lined the sides of the church, saints were clothed in gorgeous fabrics, all was decorated with ribbons, paper flowers, banners. There was a high noise level of calling back and forth, chatting and laughter.

The presidente and soon to be Imperador Captain Carvalho, resplendent in what appeared to be an admiral's uniform, was ensconced next to the altar, with him the queen and a pair of princesses, all holding decorated fans and chatting and laughing with members of the congregation. Presently the Mass began, presided over by a priest with gray hair combed close to his skull and steel-rimmed glasses glinting in the lights. I was soothed by the old Latin words enunciated in mushy Portuguese accents, soothed by old symbols and ritual melting with my visions of Eliza in her instruction with Father Flanagan, and apologetic not so much to my Savior as to my mother for not being a better Catholic.

The Festa royalty sat in a kind of pyramid, Captain Carvalho at the apex, with Isabella da Costa a head lower, her crown surmounted with the white dove, and below them the princesses in sparkling white gowns. Their cloaks, displayed over the backs of their chairs, electrified the dim air with reds, blues, and gold, embroidered with crowns, flowers, stars, garlands. Isabella was mystically beautiful beneath her complicated headdress, cheeks aglow, pink lips, dark eyes glancing right and left, tugging at a handkerchief between her hands. Carvalho gazed more serenely out on the congregation, hair slicked back so that it gleamed in the candlelight, brushing at his moustache from time to time as the priest intoned the Latin phrases, waved his censor, turned and re-turned.

When the Mass was over I waited with the crowd outside for the Imperador's party to come out. Peavine had disappeared. Captain Carvalho led the three young women down the steps; a servitor held up a tall banner with an embroidered likeness of Queen Isabel on it, four men supported a bobbing statue of her, others the magnificent capes. Now the celebrants reversed themselves to troop back to the Portuguese Hall, where the famine-ending heavenly smelling meal was to be produced. There was also a general redolence of wine and sweaty humanity. The bands of music celebrated, with offbeat tootling and drum throbbing.

From a height of ground near the hall, in the powerful odor of the meat soup, I watched the band preceding the beautiful old barouche with its team of matched grays bearing the Imperador's party through the massed cheering crowds toward me, the Imperador and the queen on the higher seat, waving their greetings, the three princesses below and facing them. Three boys holding up white paper doves swooped past me. Drunken fishermen in Sunday suits gesticulated and staggered.

Elbowing and excusing himself, hat cocked on his head, Bierce joined me. We stood together watching the progress of the barouche.

"What a grand popish nonsense!" Bierce said.

"Not to the faithful," I said.

He showed me a fan of four naughty photographs. "These are for sale," he said. "A Portuguese fellow with a fine velvet cap!"

"Any of them of Tessie Powers?" I asked.

"These seem to be of an older vintage."

"The terrible rooster?"

"None."

The barouche came abreast of us. I saw Carvalho catch sight of us. There was a moment when it seemed that he and Bierce communicated above the heads of the crowd. Bierce raised his hat. Captain Carvalho rose. Short though he was, he looked every inch a president of the Festa if not an Imperador. He removed his naval cap, and bowed deeply to Bierce in some kind of message or promise that I did not understand.

The barouche edged on past us, as did the band's music with its heavy drumbeat. Carvalho gazed straight ahead now, Isabella glancing in surprise at me.

"A fine, fine little fellow in his preposterous role," Bierce said.

Beside me a voice chirped a greeting, and here was Tessie Powers beneath a bright Chinese parasol, in a vivid blue gown with a lace collar, her pretty face pink-cheeked and pink-lipped.

"Hello, Miss Powers. Is Mr. Hearst here with you?"

"Oh, he is in the City—some new grand idea! But I came out to see these festivities."

"Will you join us for tea, Miss Powers?" Bierce said.

Her round blue eyes looked anxious, but she assented. Abandoning the festivities, the labors of the enthusiastic bands, and the dancing of the Chama Rita, we took a hack back to Old Town, and climbed steps to the hotel on the ridge above the esplanade.

At the tea table Miss Powers sat on a wicker settee with her little hands, in mesh fingerless gloves, knitted together. Tea was ordered. Bierce was at his most courtly.

"Miss Powers, you will recall the day aboard the *Aquila* when we saw Frank Stone in his launch."

"We have seen him again," she whispered. I could see the rise and fall of her bosom sheathed in blue silk.

The waitress brought a tray and distributed cups and saucers. Tessie poured the tea.

When the waitress had gone she sat straight-backed looking at Bierce levelly.

He said, "Mr. Hearst is mistaken when he says Frank Stone left Harvard because of his father's financial difficulties. He left because it was discovered that he had been performing an entrepreneurial function furnishing young women to his classmates."

Tessie looked as though it took her a moment to absorb his language. She blinked her eyes and compressed her lips.

"One of the women was named Eliza Lindley," I said.

"I am acquainted with Miss Lindley!" she said.

"According to Miss Lindley, Frank Stone was a very handsome and charming young man, who had an almost hypnotic power over the young women who worked for him."

"I believe that is true, Mr. Redmond."

Bierce said, leaning forward holding his teacup, "Is it also true that he recruited his young women by claiming to be able to assist them in a stage career?"

"That is also true, Mr. Bierce."

"I do not employ the term 'evil' lightly, Miss Powers. But young Stone's father was as close to evil as a mortal man can be. He owned a shipping line that for years imported Chinese children as slaves to the most despicable of masters. There is little doubt that his was a double trade, and that American young women were transported as white slaves to South America. Fortunately the elder Stone was indeed mortal, and died hideously for his sins. But we think that the younger Stone has been working to revive his father's lucrative ventures in white slavery and pornographic photographs at least, in conjunction with the dominant tong in Chinatown, of whom his father was also an associate. And that, Miss Powers, may be the reason that Captain Larkyn, Jasper Billings, and Jack Croft were murdered."

She was shaking her pretty head. "I must protest that Jasper Billings was not that kind of person, sir!"

"His murder was an error. There was another photographer."

She wet her lip again, sitting silently with her blue eyes flicking from one to the other of us.

"Have you had any contact with Frank Stone lately?"

She shook her head hard.

"Have you had any *communication* with him?"

"Yes, sir."

"May we ask what that communication was?"

She was a long time responding. With a sigh, she said, "Mr. Bierce, I suspect you know a good deal more about my life than I am pleased for you to know. At one time I had an involvement with Frank Stone. I thought I had the fondest affections for him, but those affections were betrayed. I no longer feel them to the slightest degree. Frank Stone is the kind of man who cannot face such a change in attitude about himself." She stopped.

"He would like you to come back to him," I said.

She frowned at me as though the question was in bad taste.

"And you of course refused," Bierce said. "Whereupon—"

She nodded vigorously. "He has photographs of me!"

"Stolen from Billings's collection?" I said.

"I'm afraid not all, Mr. Redmond." She colored darkly and turned her face down. "There were others. I am to try to persuade Mr. Hearst to change the *Examiner*'s attitude toward the masters of Chinatown, or they will be made public."

"And you told Mr. Hearst of this."

"Of course I did!"

"Do you think they will actually be made public, to the embarrassment of Mr. Hearst?"

"I don't know," she whispered. She gathered together her reticule and the folded parasol. "Please excuse me, gentlemen. This meeting has been very trying for me. I am quite exhausted by it."

We were on our feet in an instant.

Bierce said, "Miss Powers, Mr. Redmond and I must come to Sea Point to ask Ah Sook a few questions. We will not disturb you."

"Of course," she whispered. She declined my offer to fetch a hack for her, and hurried from our presence.

"I believe she is a truthful little person," Bierce said. "But Mrs. Hearst will never accept her."

"Too bad," I said.

"Shall we brave the papist hordes again? It may salve your feelings to know that I consider them superior to Protestant hell-pelters and Lazarus-rousers."

"You have questions for Ah Sook?" I said.

"I believe he knows the whereabouts of the photographic plates."

———

We sat with an uneasy Ah Sook on the veranda at Sea Point. Tessie Powers was not in evidence.

"No, I don't take!" Ah Sook insisted.

"There is no one else who could have taken them, Ah Sook. Come, you will not be punished. I guarantee it."

"No! Ah Sook do not!"

"Tell us why," Bierce said.

Ah Sook raised his chin to meet Bierce's gaze defiantly, but finally he hung his pigtailed head.

"You no tell Misser Hearse?"

"I will not," Bierce said. "Where are they?"

"I have safe place."

"I suggest that you put them somewhere Mr. Billings might have hidden them, and find them there."

Ah Sook was weeping, and he dashed his wrist across his eyes to dry them. "Try help!" he said.

"Who contacted you?"

"China man from San Flancisco! Tong man. They say hurt Missy Powee if I no bring picture-plate! I give one picture, and say no can find plate!"

"Where did you take it?"

"Take place Chinatown."

"They wanted more of them?"

"They want glass plate! I say no can find, Misser Billing lock up, hide. They say hurt Missy Powee, they say hurt my brother in Stockton, they say hurt Ah Sook. But I say no can find more!"

"Good man, Ah Sook! Now you must arrange for them to be found. Mr. Hearst is very worried about them."

"Ah Sook know that!"

"Do it!"

"Yes, do that. Thank you, thank you, misser!"

And on that afternoon of celebration in Sausalito, with fireworks bursting against the sky, Bierce and I took the ferry back to the City.

———

It was dark when I returned to Sacramento Street. Standing in a pool of light under the standard across from my rooming house was Frank Stone, wearing a black overcoat and a soft hat. I realized that I was staring at him a moment too long just as there was the hiss of a slung shot, and my head burst. I struggled to breathe as the acrid stink of chloroform filled my nostrils, and strong arms caught me as I fell.

CHAPTER TWENTY-TWO

DARING, n. One of the most conspicuous qualities of a man in security.
— *The Devil's Dictionary*

SUNDAY–WEDNESDAY, JUNE 6–9, 1891

Pitch-dark space, sense of enclosure, a whiff of maritime dead fish, salt, mold, and rust, a rocking with a little slap of sound. My head ached. Before I opened my eyes I knew exactly where I was.

I lay spread-eagle on the bed I remembered, staring up into darkness, where window rectangles were less pitchy. Sometimes the rocking was stronger, other times almost gone. The bay. The *Oliver Ferris,* of course. The room with no inside latch. Chilled, I gathered myself into a ball. My head ached. I slept.

Morning light and shadow. Sitting on the bed surveying the contents of the cabin, I wondered if South America was the destination Frank Stone planned for me. Or Canton. I was less terrified of being shanghaied to Canton or Panama than of making the trip on this rusty old ruin, which was presently bound for rehabilitation, according to Mammy Pleasant. There were tales of shanghaied men a year trying to return, years. I would have been more terrified if I were a woman bound for a Valpariso hell.

Frank Stone's connection with the tongs oppressed me, as though the Chinese knew of evil dispensations white villains could not know.

I spent time seated on the edge of the bed, listening. I could hear only the small slap of wavelets, feel the gentle rocking, sense the tide changing direction, the *Oliver Ferris* swinging on her anchor chain.

I searched the room as I had searched it once before. The rooster-head mask was in its drawer where I had seen it before, rank with implications.

There was a clatter of footsteps, the door was flung open, and a man in a kind of black dress with a flat-brimmed black hat on his head ducked in under the lintel. He had a revolver in his hand and a scowling Asian devil face. Behind him was Frank Stone.

I sat on the edge of the bed, facing them.

"Hello there, my friend," Stone said. He wore a striped suit with a flourish of rose-colored tie. His yellow hair was combed into a careful helmet, his narrow moustache twitched above his smile. He had peculiar cocked almond-shaped eyes, and cheeks as smooth as a girl's. He was a handsome devil. *I will love you till I die.*

"Slept well?" he inquired.

Where am I bound?"

"Shanghai if you are fortunate, Redmond. If the proper accommodations are made. Shanghai or Canton. The Pearl River. Frankie has never been there himself, but they say it is very fine country there."

The big highbinder stood beside the door, revolver aimed at my belly, breathing asthmatically. Past Frankie in the doorway was the bay with a glint of sun on the water, and an edge of Alcatraz.

Stone said something in Chinese and disappeared. The highbinder shoved the revolver muzzle at me.

Frankie reappeared, lugging a camera and tripod. He set these up inside the door, peering through the camera with a black cloth covering his head. He disappeared and returned with a little tray with a handle beneath. I knew what it was—a magnesium flare to take my portrait.

"What's this?" I said.

"Pose your hands up on either side of your face. That's the signal so she'll know I'm taking this photo just now."

"What for?"

"Show you're alive. Doesn't trust Frankie. Told her I'd send you to China if she'd be reasonable. China or hell, you understand. Show I have you in hand."

"You—"

Bierce would have had the vocabulary.

A young man in a big hat with a face like a choirboy. "So you were the photographer," I said.

When Stone set a match to the magnesium, it went off with a whoosh and blinding flare.

"How's your speed launch?" I said. "Do you think you will ever catch the *Aquila*?"

"Frankie will catch up to the *Aquila* and everything else," he said calmly.

"Junior devil," I said.

He frowned slightly, as though he had just remembered something, and spoke in Chinese again. The highbinder stepped forward and whacked me on the side of the head with the revolver barrel as I tried to dodge. It was all I could manage to maintain an upright position. When I had my senses back, the two of them were gone, the door shut. I used a corner of sheet to stanch the blood.

They had left a jug of water behind. I sniffed it carefully before I drank.

———

Later that day the Chinese gunman returned with a bucket of cold rice. A day passed, and another, a third, while I wondered with varying degrees and focuses of anxiety what accommodations were being made, or not.

Then the two of them were back, the highbinder with the revolver, Stone lifting and settling the big camera on its tripod. This time I was to shade my eyes with one hand, and hold the other flattened beneath my chin. The magnesium flashed painfully.

"How are accommodations progressing?" I was shocked that I could even think of joking about my situation, Eliza's situation.

I remembered Bierce replying to a fellow who disapproved of irony. "Tell me," Bierce had said, "when they stand you up before a firing squad for your good deeds, not your sins, what mode can you employ in your last speech but the ironic?"

"You're not dead yet, my friend," Frankie said. "That must tell you something."

I was fascinated by his eyes, as no doubt a trail of women had been similarly fascinated. Besotted, Eliza had said. They were black and intense. They were Oriental eyes.

Jabez Stone and a slave girl. Willie Hearst had called Frankie "Chink Stone."

"Frankie's not used to being truckled with," he said, frowning. "This'll do it or won't."

When he had gone, I thought of the rooster-head mask.

I opened the drawer, took out the contraption, and donned it. It was cool to my cheeks, with the urine stink of badly tanned leather. The smell and confinement produced a slight nausea. My vision was through an open rectangle about four inches by an inch and a half. I could see straight ahead but not up or down.

I peered around the cabin with jerks of my head. There was no mirror but I imagined I looked horrific enough. When I stripped down to my long johns I must have looked even more so. I sat on the edge of the bed in my underwear and rooster mask, staring at the door through my eye slot, willing it to open.

Time passed. There were sounds, the rap of footsteps. As the door opened I sprang toward it. I had a narrow glimpse of the highbinder's horrified face. He screamed. As I lit out for freedom I tripped over the high sill of the door and sprawled full length on the deck.

I lay there groaning. I felt as though every bone in my body was broken. My mask was snatched off. Frankie and the Chinese stood over me with their revolvers aimed at my head.

"What did you think you were going to do, fool?" Frankie said in a voice thick with anger. "Swim back to the City?

"Frankie'd be right on top of you," he went on. "In the launch. Frankie'd just hold your head down, like this."

He pressed on the back of my head, not hard, mashing my cheek against the greasy deck.

"Like this," he said again, pushing on my head, not hard. "Like this," he said, pushing again. "That'd about do it." He took his hand off my head.

"Get up, fool!"

The highbinder grasped me under the arms and I managed to gain my feet.

"Back inside!"

I was pushed back inside. I felt despair like a bottomless black hole.

There was a bump and jar. Something had collided with the *Oliver Ferris*.

"What's that?" Frankie cried out. The highbinder shouted in shrill Chinese.

An explosion so vast it seemed the earth must have dissolved flung me back across the bed to the floor beyond, the ship lurching upward with a shrieking of metal.

The doorway stood empty and open to the bay as the *Oliver Ferris* rocked wildly. Hand against the bulkhead, I steadied myself, and lit out for freedom again. Outside there was no sign of Frankie or the Chinese. The deck was hot beneath my bare feet. There were flames, the ship afire!

"Redmond!"

Frankie stood on the far side of the deck against a chain railing there. His yellow hair was mussed, but even in a position of tension he managed to look as graceful as a dancer. He held his revolver aimed at me.

"Is this your doing, damn you, Redmond?" He squinted down the barrel of his weapon.

A sheet of flame surged up beneath his feet and engulfed him. He disappeared.

The deck was burning, flames leaping all around me.

I ran toward the bow, and started back, but the deck spat flames. I hurled myself over the side.

————

I was treading water in the bay again, no cork vest this time. Against dark clouds over the eastern shore flames leaped like antic figures about the *Oliver Ferris* which sat low in the water now, fifty yards away. Evening was coming on. I clutched a plank that nudged me gently, watching the hell-ship flame and sink lower.

Lights over a dim shape of hull approached from the west with a steam engine racket, a launch. I waved an arm. The launch passed as I shouted, the wake splashing up in my face. It circled back.

Charles Peavine's bearded visage peered over the side at me. He leaned down to grasp my arm, and I surged up over the side to sprawl on the deck at his feet.

"Looking for Rudy," he said. "And here you are. Keep circling round!" he called to the man at the wheel. The putting of the launch came more rapidly. The deck slanted in a turn as we continued on.

I sat on an edge of railing, soaked and panting.

"They had me cooped up aboard. Something blew us up."

"Rudy," Peavine said. "Bound to blow up that hell-ship hulk. Rattled the windows in Sausalito. I knew right off what it was. He must be here somewhere."

"You could look for Frank Stone while you're at it."

He grunted gloomily. "Soon be too dark to see anything."

I explained my presence aboard the *Oliver Ferris,* Peavine slapping a hand on his knee. He was worried about his friend Carvalho. "Show up, Rudy!" he commanded.

The superstructure of the hell-ship still danced with flames, low to the water. The launch curved around her in broad and narrow circles. No Rudy Carvalho, no Frank Stone or the highbinder, but a sargasso sea of planks from the fishing boat that had rammed the hell-ship and blown itself up. We hove to while Peavine flashed the bull's-eye lantern over the waterlogged mess.

The *Oliver Ferris* sank with a long whisper of sound, the last flames extinguished.

We continued our rounds, Peavine in the bow with the lantern. He had furnished me with a blanket to wrap myself in.

A long time later he came back to where I reclined still shivering in the cabin.

"I believe he blew himself up with his load of dynamite. How could he be that *stupid?*"

"Maybe he wasn't," I said.

———

Back in Sausalito I telephoned the *Examiner* to send a messenger to Miss Eliza Lindley at the Stockton Street Mission to tell her that that Mr. Redmond was alive and well.

CHAPTER TWENTY-THREE

BRIDE, n. A woman with a fine prospect of happiness behind her.
— *The Devil's Dictionary*

WEDNESDAY, JUNE 9, 1891

The parlor windows at Sea Point looked out from a blaze of electric light onto the darkness of the bay, dots and smears of light on the San Francisco shore, the eastern hills blocked by the humped mass of Angel Island. We sat in a variety of chairs—white wicker, straight-backed chairs brought in from the adjoining room, the settee, Willie's master chair facing the windows: Bierce, Willie Hearst, Tessie Powers (with little boots set together primly and hands folded) on the settee, Charles Peavine, and me, still shivering and freshly shaven, in dry trousers and a shirt and too-tight jacket provided by Willie Hearst, in my stocking feet.

Willie had already been notified by Ah Sook, who was not in evidence, that the missing photographic plates had been found in a location that somehow had been missed.

Bierce stood gazing out the window at the encompassing dark, hands gripped together behind him.

"Where's the story, Mr. Bierce?" Willie said from his chair, long legs stretched out before him. His nose bisected his face straight as an arrow, prim little mouth tucked beneath the fair moustache.

"I do not want all the story printed," Bierce said without turning.

"You and Mr. Redmond have been working on this story for the *Examiner* for a month."

"You also do not want all the story printed, Mr. Hearst."

Tessie stirred on the settee, pretty face pointed toward Willie, who remained silent, frowning like a fog bank.

"I will only divulge the facts if it is my decision to print the story or not, or what of it may be printed."

"Very well, Mr. Bierce," Willie said without hesitation.

Charles Peavine leaned forward in his straight chair, scratching fingers through his beard.

"About your acquaintance at Harvard, 'Chink Stone,'" Bierce said to Willie, "whom we may assume perished with the *Oliver Ferris.*"

"Yes."

Tessie had turned her face down.

"In its time the *Oliver Ferris* brought in slave girls from China, but it was a triangular trade as well. Young American women were, as it were, shanghaied to service in South American brothels."

"That old scoundrel!" Peavine started, and stopped, leaning back with a glance at Tessie.

"Your fellow yachtsman Captain Larkyn knew Jabez Stone well. Larkyn seduced the young women who came over from San Francisco for festivities on the British yachts in the harbor below me with stories of his acquaintance amongst the producers of theatricals in this and other cities. And his mate Jack Croft was a participant, of course.

"Part of the seduction consisted in having the young women

remove their clothing for photographs which would be sent out to enhance their careers. Some of the young women balked at this course. Others did not. We know that photographs were taken aboard the *Oliver Ferris*. And we know there was a rather luxurious cabin aboard where there was no latch on the inside of the door." He halted for a breath.

"Go on, Mr. Bierce," Willie said, leaning forward.

"Terrible things happened within that room," Bierce proceded. "Some of the young women imprisoned there were fated for a terrible servitude.

"These matters led to the murders of Captain Larkyn and his mate Croft, and the photographer Billings, and ultimately to the death of Frank Stone himself by the hand of a righteous man."

There was a library hush.

Peavine rose. "What you are saying is that it was Rudy Carvalho who did the deeds. He is not here to defend himself, man!"

Bierce faced him. "Captain Peavine, did you know that Carvalho intended to sink the *Oliver Ferris*?"

"He spoke of it. I didn't take him seriously. When I heard the explosion I figured what it was."

"Would he have chosen a time when he knew Frank Stone was aboard?"

"As you know, he kept an eye on that hulk," Peavine said, seating himself again.

"Captain Carvalho was the president of the Portuguese festival, was he not?" Willie said. "Or emperor. I believe they crown an emperor!"

"The presidency is the key," Bierce said, addressing himself to Willie. "For the president is responsible for the well-being of the Portuguese community for his term of office. Captain

Carvalho knew that a previous queen of the festival had disappeared, and he suspected the cause, incorrectly as it has been revealed. And there was also an attempt to seduce *his* queen."

Peavine said, "Was Flora Rodrigues—"

"She is alive and well and her whereabouts known. Others were not so lucky. Carvalho set out to correct this bleeding sore. He shot Larkyn and brained Croft. Who is to say it was not well deserved? Who is to say Captain Carvalho is not a hero?"

No one spoke.

"But he made a mistake," I said.

Bierce nodded to me. "It is the weakness of vigilante justice."

"Poor Mr. Billings," Willie murmured.

Bierce continued. "Carvalho thought Jasper Billings was the photographer responsible for the unclothed photographs. And indeed Billings had taken nude photographs, of Miss Powers, and the young man James Dix. At least one of those photographs had come into Captain Larkyn's possession.

"And because Captain Carvalho was a man of great honor, when he realized his mistake he knew that his life was forfeit."

"Frank Stone was the photographer," I said.

"So Rudy blew himself up," Peavine said unhappily. "Poor fellow! He was a prince of a man."

"He was a president of a man," Bierce said.

"So you let him finish out his glory. What were you going to do then?"

"I don't know," Bierce said.

"How did you come to this understanding, Mr. Bierce?" Willie Hearst asked.

"I suspected him when the lists of invitations and actual appearances, and Captain Peavine's estimate of who would appear at Larkyn's ball, had been perused. Carvalho was invited, it was assumed he would come, but he was not on Mrs. Grayling's list of appearances. I knew he was the murderer of Larkyn as soon as I connected the murder with the disposal of the dead whale."

"What was that, Mr. Bierce?" Willie said. "I do remember hearing of some such event over at New Town."

"Carvalho took the responsibility of ridding the community of the dead whale. Larkyn was a similar corruption."

"Why, this is a gee-whiz story!" Willie said. "I don't see why—"

Bierce interrupted him. "There is more to it, Mr. Hearst. Young Stone was a ladies' man of multiple triumphs. He is the kind of ladies' man who could not bear to lose his power over the women of—may I say his harem?" He did not look at Tessie as he said this.

"One of these women is an acquaintance of Mr. Redmond's. Young Stone went to extraordinary efforts to persuade her to return to the fold. He had Mr. Redmond kidnapped and the young woman threatened with his death if she did not surrender."

"Oh! Oh!" Tessie whispered.

"Mr. Redmond was discovered to be the author of a series of pieces Annie Laurie rewrote on the slave girls of Chinatown," Bierce went on. "This was an embarrassment to young Stone, who sought to replace his father in tong graces."

Tessie said suddenly, "Mr. Stone threatened to reveal that he and I were acquaintances in Cambridge if I didn't prevail on Mr. Hearst to cease the Chinatown series."

"With a clumsily fabricated photograph" Bierce said.

"Yes!"

"See here!" Willie said. "I say! What cannot be printed?"

"This last untidy business cannot," Bierce said. "Surely you understand why! Miss Powers is quite vulnerable, as is Miss Lindley. Nor do I wish to tarnish the memory of Captain Carvalho. If you insist, the story can be written of the blowing up of the *Oliver Ferris,* and the fact that the president perished in the commission of that good work."

"We'll do that, then, Mr. Bierce," Willie said reluctantly. "But I protest that this is not *Examiner* journalism!"

And so it was settled, and I excused myself to take the evening ferry back to San Francisco, wearing a pair of Jasper Billings's bluchers, heading for the Protestant Mission on Stockton Street.

————

Under the sign I CAN DO ALL THINGS THROUGH CHRIST WHICH STRENGTHENETH ME, Eliza's desk and chair were empty, illuminated by the single electric bulb on its twisted cord. Miss Cochran's cubicle was also empty, but there were sounds as of a crowd of people from the commons room upstairs.

The door was ajar on indeed an assembly, a female voice droning. I slipped inside and into an empty chair. All the children were present, the little ones from the Sausalito picnic, but older ones also in their white dresses, including Miss da Costa seated in front of a table with Eliza in her blue dress, along wih a number of other people: Miss Cochran sat next to Eliza, and there were two or three older women, one of whom was at a lectern speaking—the board. Attorney Wing Ho and his bride-to-be or not-to-be Fah Loo were seated together at the end of the table.

It must have been Mrs. Chumley, president of the board, who was speaking, a plump matron with a red face, a fluff of gray hair, and a hand with an extended finger that pumped up and down like a metronome. She was complimenting Eliza's work at the Mission.

And Eliza saw me, where I sat, and crossed herself. *Crossed herself!* And then I saw Father Flanagan's bald tonsure in the front row with Miss da Costa, and Matthew Fenton.

Mrs. Chumley droned on. It was hot in the room. Exhaustion came down on me like a warm mattress. What did Mrs. Chumley mean, "Ohio"? I jerked awake. Now an older, skinny man in a frock coat was praising Eliza. What was it about? Little girls gaped back at me with grave faces under gleaming black hair.

Eliza caught my eye again and motioned with a finger, meaning she would see me in my rooms. Bending so as to conceal myself, I rose, and crept out of that hot place. In the cool of Stockton Street I breathed deeply and my senses revived.

In my rooms, seated at my typewriter wondering what it was I should be writing, I waited in a state of exhaustion and anticipation that had me shivering again.

———

When her quick rap sounded, I almost upset the typewriter table getting to the door to open it.

I swept her into my arms and inside. "You are safe!" she said in a voice muffled by my shoulder. "Thank the Lord you are safe! *Thank you!*"

We tore at each other's clothing. In bed we made love, and slept, and waked to make love again. Eliza wept, and prayed kneeling beside the bed—for what reason was not divulged, for we scarcely spoke—and we made love again. We lay in the darkness flank to flank, my arm under her head.

"What did that speaker mean, 'Ohio'?"

It was a long moment before she responded. "I go to Ohio tomorrow."

"Why *Ohio*? Why *tomorrow*?"

"Because you are safe."

"Tell me what you mean!"

"Is he truly dead?"

"We cruised the area for what seemed hours and found no sign of him."

"He said he would preserve your life if I would come back to him. He thought that was the choice I must make. But that is not the choice I made."

"I don't understand!"

"Tom, I have been having instruction from Father Flanagan to regain my old faith, which is your faith."

Something in my throat was swelling to choke me.

"I promised Our Savior that if He would save your life I would serve Him all my days."

"Serve Him—"

"There is a Carmelite nunnery in Bayfield, Ohio, where I will go for my novitiate."

"Wait!"

"That was my promise. That was the choice I made. He saved you, Tom, and I will do as I promised Him."

"Wait!" I said again.

"I take the train tomorrow. I have resigned from the Mission. Miss Cochran will assume my position until the board has made its decision. It was all very sudden, of course. How could it not have been? I have promised, Tom."

I groaned. I had been guarding the door against Frank Stone, and Father Flanagan had slipped in the window.

"Eliza, surely He will—"

"I have promised, Tom. I swore it!"

"I will go with you!" I said. "We will take a Pullman. Say yes!"

"You may come with me as far as Chicago. Will that suffice you, my darling?"

"Of course not," I said.

THURSDAY, JUNE 10, 1891

In the morning when I went to the *Examiner* to ask permission for two weeks off to tend to personal business, Bierce was seated in his office looking more dour than usual. He and the skull did not present a cheerful sight.

"Winnie has announced that she will wed Orlow Black," he said.

I was surprised. Orlow Black had only been employed at the *Examiner* a few weeks, a young journalist like me, of even less stature at the newspaper. "For heaven's sake why?" I asked. "He seems a modest fellow."

"He has much to be modest about," Bierce said. "It is ridiculous! She is a young person of some position. She has a personality made to order for newspaper work. I could have taught her to write, to rid herself of that fearful, sentimental style. To handle words as though they were diamonds, not pebbles. I could have moulded that malleable character into something—truly—" He stopped, at a loss for words, which was unlike him.

"I'm not sure she is so malleable," I said.

"I could have made of her something this newspaper could have been truly proud of. For herself to be proud of! That I could be proud of."

I said that Winnie Sweet must want to be a wife, not a mistress.

"A slave to a husband who is a slave to his wife! A pair of enslaved beings," Bierce said poisonously. He threw up his hands. "She is simply not the person that I had conceived her to be!"

I told him I would be out of town for two weeks, and headed for Sam Chamberlain's office, where the *Examiner* owed me some favors, to make it official.

So ended the Sausalito murders, Bierce's romance with Winifred Sweet, and, in five days time, my own with Eliza Lindley.

EPILOGUE

HISTORIAN, n. A broad-gauge gossip.
         — The Devil's Dictionary

1

After I had assisted Eliza onto a train bound for Bayfield, Ohio, and returned from Chicago to San Francisco, I did not hear from her for three months. After that we exchanged letters about once a month, but hers were queer, stiff missives with much reference to her fellow nuns, to her Savior, to Mary and the saints. I wept for the loss of that courage and resourcefulness, and dedication, and for the part of my own salvation in it. I sought consolation from Father Flanagan, who discussed Divine Will with me.

Then, due to some efforts on his part, or my prayers, all was changed. Sister Mary Joseph was transferred to a Sacred Heart School in St. Louis, where she was first a teacher and then the headmistress, and mailed me a photograph of herself, cowled and beautiful to me, looking very tall in her habit, with her folded eyeglasses suspended from a chain (and her tattooed buttock beneath her habit), surrounded by eight tiny charges in neat gingham dresses, with gleaming teeth, and braids sticking out on either side of their little heads like beribboned barbed wire. And I realized that Divine Will had placed her exactly where she belonged, not in my arms but safe among angels and archangels, plenipotentiaries and powers.

It was my turn to give thanks.

––––––

When I returned to the City I was loath even to bother to look up what had been published in the *Examiner* about the Sausalito murders.

The Firemen did not have a good season on the diamond. My mother had no prospects for a grandson.

2

Charles Peavine and the *Clio* left their anchorage at Old Town Sausalito in a general exodus of the British yachtsmen, all headed south. The *Clio,* however, steamed on to South America, where the good Charles hoped to find some of the enslaved young women in the ports along the coast still with their lives and health.

3

In a famous session in a hotel room in San Francisco, Mrs. Hearst and her young niece met with Tessie Powers and threatened and bribed her into abandoning Willie Hearst and heading back East. No doubt the $150,000 that was rumored to have changed hands was a help, and no doubt Willie's career an impetus. Willie was miserable for a time, but in the busy months that followed at the *Examiner* he recaptured his good spirits.

––––––

Shortly before she departed from San Francisco, Tessie confided in me that she and Willie Hearst had seen Frank Stone's steam launch twice on the bay after it was presumed to have sunk with the *Oliver Ferris,* but never close enough to identify who was aboard.

4

If Tessie Powers had not vanished from William Randolph Hearst's life, his mother would never have lent him the $7,500,000 that enabled him to purchase the *New York Journal* and invade New York and the national scene.

Mrs. Hearst was also to become California's greatest philanthropist, and there was good reason to rename the University of California Hearst University to rival Mr. and Mrs. Leland Stanford's Stanford University, for $10,000,000 of the Hearst fortune went to the Berkeley building and endowments funds, $21,000,000 in all to education in California.

The Hearst Corporation financed her eventual biography, which was written by Winifred Sweet Black Bonfils.

5

Hearst's *Journal* challenged his old employer Joseph Pulitzer's *World* for press domination of New York City, just as he had challenged the *Chronicle* in San Francisco. Willie Hearst almost single-handedly warmongered the Spanish-American "splendid little war," printing vilifications and lies about Spanish depredations in Cuba in order to increase circulation, and to embark the United States on its fling at imperialism.

Hearst became involved with two sisters, Millicent and Anita Willson, who were members of a troupe of dancers called the Merrie Maidens, performing in *The Girl From Paris*. It was thought he favored Anita, as Millicent was only sixteen, but it was Millicent he was to marry (at thirty-four), despite his mother's disapproval.

His career careened in power and megalomania. He craved the Democratic nomination for president but had to content himself with two terms as a New York congressman; he lumbered about amongst his acquisitions at San Simeon; and courted the movie industry with his mistress, the minor motion picture star Marion Davies. He who had begun his press life as a Jeffersonian Democrat ended it with totalitarian inclinations. The Hearst newspapers castigated Franklin Roosevelt as a Communist, praised Mussolini, interviewed Hitler, and ran articles by Goering and Rosenberg up until Pearl Harbor.

Ambrose Bierce wrote of him, in *The Devil's Dictionary*:

> *Hearst kept a diary wherein were writ*
> *All that he had of wisdom and of wit*
> *So the Recording Angel, when Hearst died,*
> *Erased all entries of his own and cried:*
> *"I'll judge you by your diary." Said Hearst,*
> *"Thank you; 'twill show you I am Saint the First" —*
> *Straightway producing, jubilant and proud,*
> *The record from a pocket in his shroud.*
> *The Angel slowly turned the pages o'er,*
> *Each stupid line of which he knew before.*
> *Glooming and gleaming as by turns he hit*
> *On shallow sentiment and stolen wit;*
> *Then gravely closed the book and gave it back.*
> *"My friend, you've wandered from your proper track:*
> *You'd never be content this side the tomb —*
> *For big ideas Heaven has little room.*
> *And hell's no latitude for making mirth,"*
> *He said, and kicked the fellow back to earth.*

Bierce said of him elsewhere that despite his superficial charm, Hearst had no real friends, "nor does he merit one, for, either congenitally or by induced perversity, he is inaccessible to the conception of an unselfish attachment or to a disinterested motive."

And yet, later in her life, when Tessie Powers was ill and

down on her luck, William Randolph Hearst provided for her support for the remainder of her days.

6

Winifred Sweet Black's campaign for Little Jim succeeded brilliantly. Over $20,000 was raised for the "Little Jim Fund," and the "Little Jim Ward" of Children's Hospital in San Francisco began its long life. Her journalistic successes were many: she voyaged to the island of Molokai to write about life in the leper colony there, she insinuated herself into the scene of havoc after the Galveston hurricane to describe its horrors, she lived among the Mormon women of Utah and wrote articles on polygamous marriages.

She did not remain married to Orlow Black long, and with Sam Chamberlain and others of the *Examiner* staff followed William Randolph Hearst to New York in 1895. However, she did not find New York to her liking and returned West, to Denver, where she married the publisher of the rambunctious *Denver Post,* Frederick Bonfils.

When the San Francisco earthquake and fire struck in 1906, she received a telegram from William Randolph Hearst with a message of only one word: "GO." She went.

7

Miss Cochran only briefly filled Miss Lindley's shoes as directress of the Stockton Street Mission. She was succeeded by the married pair Wing Wo and Fah Loo, who combined Miss Lindley's resourcefulness and attorney Duggan's legal expertise in rescuing bodies as well as saving souls.

8

Bierce briefly abandoned the City after the conclusion of the Sausalito murders and an attack of asthma, and resided in a hotel in Auburn to take advantage of the fine foothill air. He sent his weekly "Prattle" in to the *Examiner* from there, and he wrote to me: "I would rather dine in the receiving vault of a cemetery than in an American hotel dining-room. I mean a dining-room where ladies are admitted. The awful hush, the peculiar ghastly chill, the visible determination to be proper and avert the slow stroke of the rebuking eye that awaits the miscreant who laughs or speaks above his breath—"

9

From "Prattle":

MAN AND EAGLE

An Eagle was once captured by a Man, who clipped his wings and put him in the poultry yard, along with the chickens. The Eagle was much depressed in spirits at the change.

"Why should you not rather rejoice?" said the Man. "You were only an ordinary fellow as an eagle; but as an old cock you are a fowl of incomparable distinction."